AN ALPHA'S HEART

MONIQUE AND PEARSON

KASEY MARTIN

JESSICA WATKINS PRESENTS

❀ Created with Vellum

JESSICA WATKINS PRESENTS

Jessica Watkins Presents is the home of many well-known, best-selling authors in Urban Fiction and Interracial Romance. We provide editing services, promotion and marketing, one-on-one consulting with a renowned, national best-selling author, assistance in branding, and more, FREE of charge to you, the author.

We are currently accepting submissions for the following genres: Urban Fiction/Romance, Interracial Romance, and Interracial/Paranormal Romance. If you are interested in becoming a best-selling author and have a FINISHED manuscript, please send the synopsis, genre and the first three chapters in a PDF or Word file to jwp.submissions@gmail.com. Complete manuscripts must be at least 50,000 words.

1

FAMILY DYSFUNCTION

Monique sat at her mother's house wishing she was anywhere else. Her curvy body was uncomfortable in the fold-up chair she was sitting in, and she was starting to sweat her flat-ironed hairstyle out. Her heart-shaped face was marred with a frown and her plump lips were pursed in annoyance.

She was a thirty-six-year-old woman, but any time she passed the threshold of her childhood home, it was like she was transported back in time. Her mother treated her and her sister like they were still teenagers, and no matter how hard she tried, she would get sucked into behaving like one. It was a sordid dance that she didn't want any part of, so today, she'd brought her boyfriend and best friend to help keep her in check. However, that plan went to hell with gasoline panties on when her younger sister strolled in late. It wasn't her usual sour brashness that bothered Monique, though. It was the fact that Ashley had decided to act like Monique's boyfriend was the last man on earth.

If this little heffah doesn't stop pawing all over my damn man, I swear I am going to bust her ass!

"Monique. Monique! Are you listening to me?" Her mother's voice broke in, interrupting her thoughts.

"No, ma'am. I didn't hear what you said." Monique sighed as she turned toward her mother pasting on a smile. Her hickory brown complexion still shined bright in spite of her dour mood.

"I said..." her mother started with attitude, and Monique knew that her bad nerves were about to get even worse.

"Mama Carter, did you taste this apple pie? You need to try this. I think this is the best apple pie I've ever tasted," Venus, Monique's best friend and all-around savior, butted in.

"Child, of course I tried it. I made it." Mrs. Carter laughed as she batted her hand playfully at Venus.

Monique mouthed, "Thank you" to her bestie before she refocused her attention on her trifling ass sister and idiot boyfriend. Throughout dinner, her sister had been making snide remarks and comments, and her boyfriend had sat there like a mute. But now, her sister had taken her antics to a whole other level. Caressing and stroking of any part of Damon's body was downright disrespectful.

Ashley was the baby of the family, and she always seemed to think that she was entitled to everything. Monique usually overlooked her sister and her foolishness, but today, was not the day for turning the other cheek. *She's going too far.*

Monique was trying to be the bigger person. She was *always* trying to be the bigger person when it came to her sister. However, Monique was struggling with that particular task today. It also didn't help that Damon had been missing in action every weekend for the past few months and today, was the first time in forever that he'd made time to spend with her. But instead of being the dutiful boyfriend, this fool decided to just sit like a bump on a log and let her sister feel him up. *Foolishness.*

Monique had had enough, but the straw that broke the camel's back was when Ashley leaned over and whispered in Damon's ear. The two shared a little smirk, and then her sister winked and licked her lips. Monique didn't know who she would cut first, but blood was definitely going to be shed.

"Excuse me. What the hell are you doing?" Monique questioned her sister with a sneer. She tried. The Lord only knew she'd tried, but sometimes, she couldn't help but backslide. And right now, Monique was about to backslide her fist into somebody's jaw.

Ashley sat back, looked directly at Monique, and smiled.

This little bitch. Monique knew that her sister was trying to cause a scene, but for what?

"What's the matter, Moni? I can't talk to *your* man? If he was really yours, you wouldn't have to watch him so closely, would you?" Ashley's eyebrow raised and the evil smile grew. She reminded Monique of a Cheshire cat, and Monique hated fuckin' cats.

Monique opened her mouth, but before she could respond, Venus cleared her throat, gabbing Monique's attention. Venus shook her head ever so slightly and mouthed, "Don't do it." Monique took a deep breath to try and rein in her ire.

Her best friend was well aware of the tension between Monique and Ashley. They had never been close, but the older they got, the worse their relationship became.

"You can talk to whomever you chose, *Ash*." Monique held her face in a neutral expression, but when Ashley's face grew into a frown, she struggled not to roll her eyes. *This is a thirty-year-old woman. Lord, be a fence.*

Monique swore that her sister was still living as a ten-year-old, trying to antagonize her older sibling. The shit was exhausting and stupid as hell.

"Then why did you ask what the hell I was doing? Clearly, I'm having a conversation with this fine ass man beside me." Ashley grinned as she rubbed her hand down Damon's chest once again.

Damon finally had the good sense to scoot slightly out of Ashley's reach, but it was too little, too late. His ass wasn't getting away with flirting with her sister. Monique couldn't believe the audacity of either one of them. Did they think she was stupid? Did they think she would just sit there and be disrespected? *The hell I look like?*

"Ashley, baby girl, why don't you go and get your mama another drink?" their mom spoke up, trying to defuse the thick tension.

"Mama, you always want to send me running. I'm havin' a conversation. Monique can get your drink." Ashley waved her manicured hand dismissively at their mother.

Monique just shook her head. It was her mama's fault that Ashley talked to her like a dog. Their mom still treated her grown ass sister like a child, giving the woman whatever she wanted. She had never bothered to correct her disrespectful behavior or her funky ass attitude, and now, she treated their mother like shit. Monique had threatened her sister more than once behind their mama, but it looked like she was going to actually have to whoop her sister's ass.

"Damon, why don't you go get my mama a drink?" Monique posed it as a question, but it wasn't. He was in the doghouse and by the look on his face, he knew it.

"Uh, yeah, okay." Damon quickly got up out of his chair and practically ran into the kitchen.

Good. I'm glad you can see I'm not playing with yo' funky ass. Sitting up here letting my sister flirt and touch all on you. Monique's thoughts were fueling her fire. Her legs were bouncing up and down, and she started to wring her hands in frustration. She was about to explode.

Monique watched Ashley roll her eyes and cross her arms over her chest. It was seriously like dealing with a child. Arguing with her sister was stupid and beneath her, and she had to keep reminding herself that she was a grown ass woman. *I own my own business, I'm successful, I have a master's degree, and I own my own house and car. I don't need to beat up my little sister like I'm an adolescent.*

"Why'd you send him to the kitchen? You just can't stand that I can hold a man's attention and you can't." Ashley scoffed as she narrowed her eyes with resentment.

"Are you fucking ten years old? There is something seriously wrong with you," Monique stated softly, but the room was so tense and silent that everyone heard what she'd said. All of her relatives that were loud and rowdy had settled down to watch the show. Since there weren't any children under the age of eighteen, nobody moved from the table.

"Monique Renee Carter, don't you use that language at my table!"

her mother scolded. And out of respect for her mother, Monique didn't roll her eyes like the child she accused her sister of being.

"Mama, you might want to go on in the kitchen to see what's taking Damon so long with your drink," Monique responded calmly.

"Don't try to handle me, young lady. This is *my* house. I'm not going anywhere, and you're not going to talk like that to your sister in *my* house. You should do better for yourself. I'm disappointed in you." Her mother tsked, shaking her head in disgust.

Monique laughed out loud at her mother's words. She could never understand why she treated her sister like she was still a child that needed protecting instead of a thirty-year-old woman who needed to grow the hell up. She also didn't know why she treated Monique like she was the failure.

"Mama, I'm not trying to handle you. I'm trying to handle the slut puppy you raised," Monique shot back but she wasn't finished.

"Don't be dis..."

Monique held up her hand, cutting off her mother. "Stop. You let this woman come in your house and disrespect you and *me*. She talks and acts crazy, but you tell me *I'm* the disappointment." Monique pointed to herself. "Me... So, since I'm already a disappointment, let me get something else off my chest. And I want each and every one of you to listen, so you can *all* understand." She pointed at her sister. "If you keep fucking with me, I will whoop the dog shit out of you, sister or not."

"Bitch, you won't do sh..." Ashley started to stand, but her mother's words stopped her.

"Ashley Danielle, you better not get your narrow behind up out of that chair. Now, both of ya'll, shut up! I've heard enough!"

"Mama, how can you yell at me? You always do this!" Ashley yelled.

Venus snickered in the corner while she sipped on her drink, causing Monique to look in her direction with lips pursed. Venus shrugged nonchalantly.

Monique shook her head. She'd had enough of this family get together. She hated the holidays, and she knew if she stayed any longer, she would end up breaking her mama's heart by making good on her threat to beat the hell out of her sister.

Monique grabbed her purse and stood up. "Show's over, everybody. Venus, let's go."

"Where do you think you're going? We aren't finished." Mrs. Carter stood from her chair. Her tiny stature seemed big as she put her hands on her round hips and frowned.

"Yes, ma'am, we are." Monique left the house with a shamed face Damon lagging behind.

Damn Sunday dinners will be the death of me.

MONDAY MORNING WASN'T TURNING out much better than Sunday. Monique and Damon had argued for hours before she asked him to leave her house and go home to his apartment. He couldn't understand why Monique was so upset with him, and she couldn't understand how a man with a degree in engineering was so damn dense. Damon said he didn't discourage Ashley's unwanted advances because he didn't want to make a scene and embarrass her. He'd tried to convince Monique he wanted to avoid the mess that had inevitably happened, and she should thank him for his efforts. Monique told him that he should be thankful that violence wasn't her go to emotion before showing him the door.

Monique knew that they would make up eventually. They always did, but she didn't really want to discuss anything with Damon for a while. Then, first thing Monday morning, even before her alarm, her mother was blowing up her phone. Monique let it roll to voicemail, but her mother kept calling until she answered. So she'd started off her day with her mother telling her that she needed to apologize, and she continued to chastise her like she was the one who'd been wrong. Monique, the dutiful daughter, had listened, agreed, and apologized to her mother before hanging up.

Always take the high road.

~

MONIQUE HAD BEEN STUCK in traffic for the last twenty minutes on a ten-minute drive. She hadn't had her morning coffee, and her road rage was starting to show. She would need to hit the gym to work out some of the stress the past few days had caused her. There was no way in hell her clients could see their image consultant looking stressed out. She was the fixer. She didn't need to be fixed. Her façade had to be on point at all times, and any cracks could be detrimental to the business that she'd spent years building.

Monique was one of the youngest owners in the public relations business. She'd started her firm, *The Fix*, at the age of thirty and she hadn't looked back. She worked as a consultant for one of the largest public relations agencies in Texas just out of college. Monique worked her way up and landed the prestigious role of junior executive, but she'd always wanted her own firm. So as she learned the ropes, she slowly started her own business. Once her clientele expanded and it became too much to handle in her spare time, she took the plunge and ventured out. Everything had worked out and now, she was becoming competition for the firm she had left.

As she pulled into her reserved parking spot, she breathed a sigh of relief. *I made it to work on time and I managed not to ram my car into anyone else. It's the small things that matter, and I can finally get my daily dose of caffeine.* Monique smiled as she climbed out of her sensible black, four door BMW.

She walked into her small office and smiled. It wasn't a huge space or a large building, but it was *hers*, and that was what mattered. Monique knew someday she would get to the big league. She just had to keep landing those big clients.

"Hey, Shannon." Monique waved at her receptionist as she stepped through the door.

"Morning, Monique. Coffee's on your desk." Shannon smiled with a wink.

Everyone in the office knew that Monique was *not* a morning person, and coffee was a requirement.

"Thanks!" Monique replied as she hurried to her office. Before she could take her first soothing sip, her P.A., Blake busted through her door.

"You will not believe this!" Blake smiled with her brown eyes dancing with excitement.

Monique rolled her eyes. Blake was always so overly excitable. She would make a big deal when the McRib came back to McDonald's.

"What's up?" Monique asked after she finally took a sip of her coffee. She savored the taste, tuning Blake out. *Mmmmm... Caffeine.*

"He said he wants to meet with you tomorrow!" Blake's caramel complexion was red with excitement, but Monique had missed half of what she'd said.

"Who? Who wants to see me?" Monique asked.

Blake rolled her eyes. "Keifer Swanson called. He wants to meet with you about Pearson Grant."

Keifer Swanson was a former co-worker who Monique networked with from time to time. However, the name that had her heart nearly stopping was Pearson Grant. He was the owner and operator of one of the largest tech companies in the US. He was also known as one of the largest assholes in the US.

"Pearson Grant needs a fixer!" Blake yelled.

"Well, I'll be damned."

2

BUSINESS AS USUAL

2 4 HOURS EARLIER...

Some people liked to say that Pearson Grant was a megalomaniac. He liked to say *fuck* those people. He was successful. He was ruthless. He was unforgiving. He was also one of the biggest sharks in the business world. Pearson was also one of the biggest assholes you would ever meet, and that's because he genuinely didn't like people. As a matter of fact, he hated most people he came in contact with. Hence, his despicable behavior.

However, even with his general dislike for other humans, Pearson owned and operated his own multi-million-dollar company, Media Tech Innovation. And unfortunately, he couldn't just hide behind his computer. He had to interact with other humans from time to time.

Pearson would also do anything to make and keep his company successful, so that was how he'd been persuaded to do an interview with the ditzy blond sitting across from him. She was asking him asinine things that he would never know or care about. And if she asked him one more question about some social media no talent hack, he was going to lose his shit.

This was supposed to be an interview for the business segment on a nationally syndicated morning talk show. It was supposed to be quick. It was supposed to help his image. He had worked tirelessly to get to where he was today, and that was because he always did what needed to be done. So even though he was against this whole thing, he knew that in the long run it would help his company. *This shit better be worth it.*

Pearson was doing his best to play nice with *Flirty Franny,* but truth be told, he didn't have time for nice. He had shit to do. But his public relations director, Kiefer Swanson, had convinced him that doing a ten-minute segment would help garner some attention for his tech company before the opening of a new division was announced. So reluctantly, he'd agreed.

Pearson knew that it was a mistake as soon as the reporter slithered her way into his dressing room before the show. The woman was as subtle as a talking monkey. Her pre-show wardrobe consisted of a low-cut tank top and the tightest yoga pants Pearson had ever seen. Darlene Austin did everything in her power to make sure he knew she was interested on a personal level. She was seduction personified, or so she'd *thought.*

Pearson wasn't opposed to beautiful women coming on to him, but he knew that she had an agenda. Darlene was a social climber. She had been connected with several high profile men, and Pearson was not about to be the next rung on her ladder. So without any hesitation, he turned Darlene Austin down flat.

Now, Pearson sat across from Darlene and her irritating ass giggling, he definitely wished he had turned down not just her, but the interview as well. He thought that she would be more professional when they got on set, but nope, she continued her outrageous flirting.

"Do you think that celebrities have great influence on technology?" Darlene batted her long false lashes and gave a beaming smile. Pearson tried his best not to let his irritation show, so he attempted to smile.

Well, actually, Pearson really didn't smile, so it was more of a display of his teeth than a true smile. But he was relieved and slightly less annoyed because at least this question had something to do with technology.

"I think that society as a whole has influence on technology. It is as simple as supply and demand. People want the greatest and latest, and companies like mine have to make sure we keep up with the trends." Pearson tried to keep his answers clear and to the point. His voice lacked very little inflection and he kept his facial expression as neutral as he possibly could.

Darlene didn't seem to care about his cold demeanor or his lackluster responses because she continued to giggle and flirt. Pearson was surprised that she hadn't tried to mount him right on the couch the way she was behaving. *I guess a "no" doesn't matter to this woman. Despicable...*

The overzealous hostess continued to drone on with her simple ass questions and her extreme flirting, effectively exasperating Pearson to his core. He could feel his left eye starting to twitch and he knew his annoyance was starting to show.

"So, what do you think of celebrities visiting the White House? I mean our president is basically a celebrity himself, so I don't think it's unusual for big-time A-listers to want to visit, but what's your take?" Darlene flipped her blond hair over her shoulder and leaned toward Pearson like she had asked the most tantalizing question of all time. But really she had shown just how stupid she was with the president comment. *Who the fuck thinks that orange orangutan is a damn celebrity?*

It took all the will power he could muster not to snap at the dimwitted woman. But a frown crossed his handsome face before he could stop it. *This shit is not what I agreed to. I'm going to kill Kiefer.*

"I don't think about celebrities because I don't give a shi..." Pearson stopped himself from cursing and cleared his throat. "I don't bother with such trivial things. If you haven't noticed, I run a fortune 500 company." He could barely keep the growl of irritation out of his deep voice.

"Oh, well..." Darlene sat back as she cleared her throat, she obviously had finally picked up on Pearson's impatience. "It's been such a *pleasure* being in your company today. But you seemed a little put out with this interview." Darlene cocked an overarched eyebrow, and Pearson took it as a challenge.

I'm here for my image. Don't fuck it up, Pearson.

"No, I'm not at all *put out*. I mean I did take the time out of my busy schedule to come here today, so if it was an inconvenience, I wouldn't have shown up," Pearson coolly replied.

However, Miss Darlene looked as if she was ready for his response. She straightened even more in her chair as she returned Pearson's cold stare. All signs of the flirtatious desperate woman were gone. "So, Mr. Grant, why don't you tell us about your *big* successful company? Media Tech Innovation, that's the name, right?"

"I would love to tell you all about my company. I started when I was in my late twenties and I took a chance. It's not easy to have faith in yourself when others try to block your success."

"So, your business was always a success?" Darlene questioned with a smirk.

"No, I definitely struggled. I—"

"Well, it's amazing that you're so *confident*, but can admit to struggling." Darlene cut Pearson off before he could finish his statement.

He knew then that this interview was not about getting his company's name out there or the new launch. It was about Darlene making a name for herself at Pearson's expense.

"Yes, I can admit to struggling. However, since you seem dead set on cutting me off, my story is going to be in the next edition of Forbes Magazine. You can read about it along with the masses. It's where *successful* businessmen like me get recognized," Pearson responded, forgetting about his image altogether.

"Well, I heard you almost had to declare bankruptcy a few years ago. That must've been rough for someone so *successful*," Darlene continued as if Pearson hadn't addressed her behavior. Pearson could hear her condescending tone of voice and he didn't miss the hateful gleam in her not-so-innocent, hazel eyes.

Oh she thinks she's an actual journalist...

Pearson wanted to scoff at the nerve of the woman, but he held his face blank. He had plenty of experience with handling undesirable situations. This woman was a glorified gossip monger posing as a news anchor, so he could definitely handle her. If she thought she would get the best of Pearson Grant, she was mistaken. Nobody would ever get the best of him. *Ever.*

Pearson sat up, adjusting the collar on his finely-tailored shirt. He looked Darlene directly in her eyes and responded, "Sometimes, things don't go as planned, but it takes a lot of hard work and dedication to run a business. It's not like TV where all it takes is blond hair and capped teeth to make it." Pearson's expression remained a stone mask even as Darlene's face began to flush deep pink.

"Excuse you!" Darlene sneered.

"No. Excuse *you.* I have sat through this foolishness long enough. You know nothing about business, and the one business question you manage to ask is a slight against my company. *Please!* Lady, you wouldn't know what good business was if it slapped you in your over-done face."

The woman stuttered in indignation, but Pearson didn't give a damn what she was trying to say as he stormed off the set. He could see the flurry of movement in the studio and panic as they tried to figure out what to do. It was a recorded segment, and Pearson didn't care if they decided to cut the entire piece. *Airhead won't make a fool out of me.*

"Pearson!" Kiefer yelled after him before he even made it a good fifty yards away.

"Not now, Kiefer. I can't believe you talked me into this bullshit," Pearson growled as he ran his hand through his hair. His piercing eyes were filled with anger and frustration.

"This was supposed to have been helpful. I figured you could keep it together for ten freaking minutes! Man, come on!" Kiefer's blond hair was in disarray as if he had been tugging at it.

"Yeah, well it looks like you were wrong as usual," Pearson barked.

"Excuse me, gentlemen," a mousy woman spoke, trying to get their attention, but Pearson wasn't having it. He held up his hand and continued his rant.

"This shit didn't help. You better hope I don't fire your ass, Keifer! That simple-minded idiot and her stupid, fucking questions."

"Uh, Mr. Grant, can I please..." the mousy woman spoke up again, but again Pearson and Keifer kept arguing, ignoring her.

"Pearson, the stunt you just pulled could potentially do a lot of damage," Keifer argued.

"Fuck any damage! They can cut the segment! I should've never agreed to do this stupid shit. I can't believe that ditzy bimbo had the nerve to try to put me in my place. If it wasn't for her big fake tits and ass and sleeping her way to the top, she probably wouldn't have a job anyway." Pearson seethed.

"Mr. Grant!" the mousy woman yelled, finally gaining his attention.

"What? What the hell do you want?" Pearson yelled back

"You still have on your mic," the woman replied, clearly flustered.

All of the color drained from Kiefer's face, and Pearson knew that he had just made one of the biggest screw ups in his career. Not only had he just insulted the interviewer to her face, now, they had audio of him degrading her.

"Fuck!" Pearson snatched the mic off and flung it at the nervous woman. His red face displayed his fury as he stormed heatedly out of the studio to his waiting car.

∼

THE NEXT DAY, Pearson paced in front of the large windows in his office. He would usually marvel at the extraordinary view of the Dallas skyline, but today, it was a blur among his scattered thoughts.

Pearson didn't have regrets. Of course, he always thought he was right, so there wasn't any room for regrets. This time, however, he had a feeling in the pit of his stomach that warned of dire consequences for the unfortunate situation he now found himself in.

Pearson was glad that his vice president was out of the country on business. Mark Simon was high strung and tended to get stressed out easily when it came to Pearson's unpredictability. This situation would give Mark a heart attack. No matter what negative reaction Mark might have, Pearson would have to tell him what was going on, especially because it could affect the company.

The soft knock on the door brought Pearson out of his thoughts.

"Come in," Pearson called out.

"Grant, the conference room is setup and Keifer just arrived," Pearson's personal assistant, Kelsey answered.

"Thank you, Kels," Pearson responded after taking a deep breath to fortify himself for the cluster fuck he had to endure.

Pearson walked into the large spacious room, and surprise was evident on his face. He hadn't anticipated on seeing his entire legal team seated around the massive table. *Shit!*

"So I'm guessing this won't be cured with an apology then?" Pearson sighed as he took his seat at the head of the conference table.

"No, Pearson. This is much, much worse than an apology, I'm afraid," one of the head attorney's responded.

"We can't take any legal action against the station. You agreed to the interview, and you were on their property wearing their mic. It isn't slander if it is your own words they are using against you." The lawyer shook his head with a frown.

"Okay, so the recording gets out. Everyone already knows I'm an asshole. What's the problem?" Pearson didn't see how this could influence his already long-suffering image. He was a dick and he made no apologies for it. He still didn't understand what any of this had to do with his company's worth.

"The problem is our investors are starting to get antsy about your growing unpredictability. People like their investments to be stable, a controlled environment with a predictable owner and CEO that they can trust." Keifer's tone was sharp and it conveyed his growing impatience with Pearson's flippant attitude.

"Not only have I made Media Tech Innovation a multi-million-dollar success, I have made our investors multi-millionaires. Why the hell would they question the stability of the company just because I called some woman a bimbo?" Pearson was beyond frustrated with this whole thing. If he could travel back in time, he would tell Keifer to fuck right off.

"Look, a CEO that can't hold his tongue is detrimental to the image of the company. And whether you like it or not, image is a big part of the success that we have," Keifer said with finality.

"Mr. Grant, it's not only about image, but with the tone of the current umm... society, it isn't wise to align with a man that can be viewed as chauvinistic. If you are bold enough to call a woman a bimbo on tape, then what are you doing to your female employees? It just isn't positive no matter how you try to spin it," the lead attorney spoke up again.

"That is preposterous! I might be an asshole, but I am *not* a pervert. I would never sexually harass my employees, females or otherwise." Pearson could no longer hold his temper at bay. With every word from his lawyers, his temperature continued to rise.

"Be that as it may, our stocks could potentially take a dive if a scandal like this gets out, and we need a plan to combat this before it gets worse."

Pearson had to admit this was worse than he thought if his company was going to be majorly affected. He couldn't let that happen. He was still reluctant, but doing nothing wouldn't help.

"Fine. What do I need to do?" Pearson sighed, resigned to the fact that he would have to jump through hoops to get this situation under control.

Pearson watched Keifer's face break into a wide grin, and the gleeful expression made Pearson cringe.

"I have someone I would like you to meet. This person is going to help us with your *image*. And no, you don't have a choice," Keifer stated, still smiling.

Keifer rose from his seat and headed to the door of the conference room. The bad feeling that had clung to Pearson was growing rapidly. And even though he never wanted to take advice from Keifer again, he knew that he was in between a rock and a hard place. *Shit!*

What happened next was unexpected. Keifer walked back into the room with a goddess following him.

The first thing Pearson noticed was her smooth chocolate skin that looked like it would be unbelievably soft to touch. Her curvy body was draped in what had to be tailored bright cobalt high-waist slacks with a fitted white blouse tucked inside. Although the outfit wasn't tight, it fit her body to perfection. Her hair hung down past her shoulders and framed her heart-shaped face. Her kissable gloss-covered lips were pursed. Pearson knew he had been staring for an inappropriate amount of time, but he couldn't help himself.

Keifer cleared his throat, and Pearson seemed to be unable to drag his eyes away from the beautiful woman in front of him. *How is she supposed to help me?*

When Keifer cleared his throat again, Pearson knew he had gone past inappropriate into creeper territory.

So much for not being seen as a pervert.

3

FIX IT

At the look of lust on her new client's face, Monique was positive that this particular mess was going to be grueling to fix. Keifer had briefed her on the details of the situation, but she was sure that with some strategic planning, she would be able to make sure that Pearson Grant avoided the fire of public scrutiny before the story even broke. However, if he was going to be accused of being a chauvinist pig, then his inability to hide the obvious desire in his eyes for someone he just met was going to be problematic.

This is going to be hard work. Monique pursed her lips as Keifer cleared his throat for the second time.

When Pearson finally managed to compose himself, Monique took a deep uncomfortable breath. Although he was a client and his stare was inappropriate, she wasn't blind. Pearson Grant was absolutely gorgeous.

He stood slightly over six feet. His long muscular body was encased in a light grey slim-fit suit that had been clearly made exclusively for him. His golden-brown hair was cut into a short style with sideburns that blended into his five o'clock shadow. His bright green eyes, currently shining with interest stood out against his tanned olive skin. The man was a walking buffet of hotness.

Monique had to clear her own throat from the sizzling sensation his gaze had left on her skin. She had to remind herself that she had a man, she was a professional, and she was here to do a job. But she couldn't deny that Pearson Grant was beyond handsome.

"This is Monique Carter. She is an image consultant. We go way back, and I trust her implicitly. She's the best at what she does, and we need her," Keifer finally introduced her to Pearson.

By Keifer's tone of voice and his drawn-out introduction, Monique could only guess she was a "surprise" visitor.

"Miss Carter, it's a pleasure." Pearson's voice was deep and sensual, and it took more effort than Monique was comfortable with to not fan herself and purr. However, she was not new to attractive men with smoldering gazes and baritone voices, so she held her head high and got down to business.

"Mr. Grant." Monique nodded simply as she took a seat at the table. No matter what the circumstance, she was determined to make this situation a success. It would mean the world to her business. This was the huge client that she needed to become an even bigger success.

"Miss Carter has already been given the details of the situation, and her skills are necessary to keep you from the public persecution that you are inevitably about to experience," Keifer explained.

"It's been two days, and the recording hasn't even been released yet. How do we know it's going to be some catastrophic event, Keifer?" Pearson questioned, and it was Monique's distinct impression that she was an unwanted addition to this boys-only club.

"Because sweeps start in a few weeks, and this is a juicy story. There is no way they would release this gold mine before sweeps week. We have roughly three weeks to try to get ahead of this thing or you're going to be in a world of hurt." Monique had tried to convey the seriousness of the matter without being seen as dramatic. But the truth was that having gossip like this with the receipts to back it up was a reporter's dream. There was no way they were going to sit on this story.

"The teasers for the episode have already started to air. They are going to build this thing up until the public is in frenzy. Then, you, my friend, will be tried and found guilty in the court of public opinion," the lead attorney spoke up again.

"Just releasing an apology statement will not be good enough. You need an image makeover," Monique added.

She could tell by the rigid set of Pearson's jaw that he was not happy. She could see that he was grinding his teeth and his tanned olive complexion began to turn red.

"I didn't mean to... offend that woman..." Pearson began, but Monique cut him off.

"No, you didn't mean for her to *hear* you. There is a difference. You said exactly what you meant to say."

"Listen, I don't need anybody telling me what I meant." Pearson's seductive voice was now laced with contempt. Monique could tell he was a man that was used to doing and saying whatever he wanted without consequences. He was in for a rude awakening.

"Fair enough," Monique responded coolly. "But the fact of the matter is whatever you meant, what you said was clear. It was derogatory and insensitive, and an apology alone isn't going to fix it." She sat back in her chair, crossing her legs and folding her hands on the table.

"You don't mind being labeled as the bad guy, but—"

"You mean the asshole," Pearson interrupted with a raised eyebrow.

"Hmmm..." Monique hummed noncommittally before she continued. "It's okay to be aloof to the point of condescension, but being a sexist, demeaning jerk is something altogether different."

Pearson's handsome face still held a deep frown, and Monique wasn't sure if she would be able to convince him to do what needed to be done.

"So what do you suggest?" Pearson finally questioned after a tense few moments.

"First, you have to apologize," Monique stated.

"I thought you said an apology wouldn't fix it? You just lectured me about how an apology wasn't good enough." Pearson rolled his eyes, and he reminded Monique of a petulant child.

"I said an apology *alone* wouldn't fix it. We have a lot of work to do, and it starts with an apology to the interviewer, the station, women, and any person that took offense. Then you have to show that you are truly sorry. The public is tired of empty apologies. They are going to be against you, and your company *will* take a hit. But if you follow my lead, you won't stay down for long and the damage won't be permanent."

"At this point, you don't have a choice," Keifer interrupted their tense exchange.

"Fine. But if this doesn't work, mine won't be the only reputation that suffers," Pearson threatened. His face flashed with anger, and Monique couldn't help the shiver that ran down her spine. His intensity was a challenge that she knew she couldn't fail.

Monique was nobody's punk, but her reputation was on the line too, and she wouldn't mess this up.

"Threats are unnecessary. I know how to do my job, Mr. Grant. We will work on a statement, and you will post a video message for all news and social media platforms."

"Why can't I just release a written statement?" Pearson questioned.

Great everything is going to be an uphill battle. Fine. I got this.

"Because a written statement is cold and impersonal, and we are trying to get you away from that. A sincere, warm apology is what you have to give the people, so I hope you can act."

Monique caught Pearson's narrow-eyed stare at her comment, but he said himself that he was an asshole. No point in sugar coating.

The entire team spent the rest of the afternoon and well into the evening composing and recording the apology message. It took several attempts, but Pearson was able to manage a decent-looking apology. The coldness he often displayed was not an act like Monique had suspected. It was his true personality, and that was going to be a very large issue.

It's okay. I got this.

~

"*I SINCERELY APOLOGIZE to anyone that I may have offended with my off-color remarks. Ms. Darlene Austin was simply doing her job and in no way shape or form did she deserve my callous remarks...*"

Monique watched the replay of Pearson's recording for what seemed like the millionth time. The media outlets were all a buzz with the unapproachable tech genius' unusual forthcoming message. The comments so far had been mixed, but the overall consensus was that apologizing was the step in the right direction.

All she had to do now was get Pearson to follow instructions and keep his mouth shut for the rest of the business quarter, and his company and his reputation should be in the clear. *Easier said than done.* Monique had only spent a few hours with Pearson, and she already knew that the next couple of months were going to test her in every way possible.

Monique sighed as she pulled up to her home. It had been a long day, and all she wanted to do was kick off her shoes, have a nice, warm bath, a glass of wine, and relax. She had another grueling day ahead of her, and exhausted wasn't even the word to describe how tired she was.

As she sat soaking in her large claw-foot tub, Monique's phone rang. She almost didn't answer it when she saw Damon's name flash across the screen, but they hadn't had a real conversation since their argument three days earlier.

"Hello?" Monique answered trying not to let the attitude she was feeling come through in her voice.

"Hey, babe," Damon responded cheerfully.

Monique rolled her eyes. He always did the same thing. They would argue about something he'd done, he would ghost her for a few days, and then come back like nothing had ever happened. The problem was Monique continued to let him come back without correcting what he'd done or addressing the issues they were having. *Circle of dysfunction.*

"What is it, Damon?" She sighed, exasperated with not only him but herself as well.

"I know you're not still mad. I don't want your sister. You need to stop being so insecure and realize you have a good man." Damon's words were like a slap in the face.

Monique sat up quickly, sloshing water onto the floor. Her relaxation had officially been interrupted. *This motherfucker!*

"You need to realize that insecurity has nothing to do with feeling disrespected. You know how Ashley is. We've been dating for two years now. Letting another female flirt and touch you without saying anything is disrespectful no matter *who* the woman is."

"Well, she's *your* sister. Why are you trying to correct me when you need to be correcting her?" Damon snapped.

"Please believe that I already had a conversation with Ashley and now I'm telling you. Either you can understand and we can move forward or you can stay oblivious and I can move on. It's your choice, Damon." Monique's voice was calm, but her temper was boiling beneath the surface.

"Baby, baby, listen. It's not that serious. I understand what you're saying." Damon had backtracked so fast that Monique thought she would get whiplash. "I'm not interested in your sister. You know that. Why don't I take you out tomorrow? We can have a nice relaxing dinner and reconnect."

His words always sounded good, but Monique had to break the cycle. This was it. If it didn't work this time, she had to be done. Two years was enough time to get their shit together.

"Okay, but I'll be busy this week with a big client. How about we do something this weekend?"

"Uh... uh... Wow, this weekend?" Damon stammered.

"If you have plans then we don't have to do anything." Monique had begun to get suspicious way before Damon's little display at Sunday dinner. He had made an excuse on why he couldn't see her for the past several weekends. Last Sunday was the first time in weeks that he had made time for her on the weekend.

"No, this weekend is fine. I'll plan something and let you know," Damon finally responded.

"Okay then. I need to go. It's been a long day and I'm tired. I'll talk with you later." Monique disconnected the call before she changed her mind about giving him another chance.

The next few days were going to be tedious, and she had to make sure that she brought her A game. Unfortunately, her relationship or what was left of it, would have to take a back seat for now.

MONIQUE HAD BEEN in her office since six that morning. She was on her third cup of coffee and her progress was slow going. Pearson Grant may have been a dismissive jerk, but after interviews with heads of all of his departments, including his human resource manager, at least there weren't any suspected harassment from any of his employees. That was the good news. The bad news was that in his personal life, he tended to treat women like a smorgasbord of play things.

Monique disconnected yet another call with one of Pearson's "female companions." To be fair, none of the women had been paid or had an involuntary relationship with Pearson. But there were certainly no sentiments of undying love.

It was the same story over and over from multiple women. Pearson would show interest, wine and dine them, sex them, and leave them. The relationships would last a few months, and he would send them a parting gift of jewelry and flowers with a card saying their time had come to an end.

Nothing he did was against the law, and his reputation as an asshole would remain firmly intact. However, if there was a scorned lover out there, they definitely would be back at square one in the court of public opinion. So, Monique had to now question the very abrasive asshole that was her client.

Shit!

Although Pearson obviously didn't give a damn about his image,

Monique had a feeling he would not want his personal life under the microscope.

"This is part of the job, Moni. Suck that shit up," Monique coached herself, but she knew the task was going to be rough.

It's okay. I got this! Monique repeated her mantra in her head.

4

HELP NOT WANTED

"Hmmm. Yes! Pearson, give it to me!" Pearson's latest companion, Stacy, screamed loudly.

Pearson needed to get his mind off of everything in his life. He needed to get lost in mindless no-strings-attached sex. However, Pearson's head wasn't exactly in the game, and Stacy was trying a bit too hard to gain his attention. And when one of his companions couldn't keep his attention, it was time for a new one.

Stacy knew her time was coming to an end, and she was doing her best to stay relevant and in Pearson's bed. And just like all of the ones before her, Stacy thought laying it on thick and clinging to Pearson for dear life would extend her time. It wouldn't. It never did.

"Shut up. Head down ass up, Stacy," Pearson growled as he slapped her pale ass, turning it red. She moaned loudly and without further prompting, she did what she was told.

Pearson pumped with a steady rhythm. But the long-legged red head writhing beneath him was not who he pictured. In fact, the only woman on his mind was the curvy russet-skinned beauty who had walked into his office the day before and turned his world upside down.

Pearson could feel his member becoming harder with just the

thought of her. She wasn't a direct employee, but unfortunately, they were going to be working closely for the next few months and he wouldn't take another hit to his so-called "image" again. His lack of caring was what had gotten him into this mess in the first place.

If Pearson didn't hear the word image for the rest of his life, it wouldn't be good enough.

Stacy's loud moans brought Pearson back to the moment. He could feel how wet she was even through the condom he was wearing. He continued his pace, his strokes getting deeper with each thrust of his hips.

Stacy screamed her pleasure, panting out nonsensical words. Pearson had to admit that Stacy was a beautiful woman. She was just his type; a party girl with nothing better to do than to be his lover from time to time. She had long hair, bright blue eyes, a tall, slim frame with legs that went on forever and porcelain skin. As attractive as she was, she was interchangeable with the rest of Pearson's female companions. The only difference between them was the hair color.

However, Monique Carter was different. Her curves were compacted to precision in her succulent body. Pearson was obsessed with her hickory-colored skin and expressive brown eyes. He could tell she was passionate about her job, and no one could deny her intelligence; which made him want her that much more.

He could imagine his large hands caressing her soft skin. Rubbing and touching every inch of her, indulging in the weight of her breasts in his hands, and how her nipples would pebble at the feel of the feather soft flick of his fingers.

"Fuuuuck!" Pearson groaned as he sped up once again. He pumped his swollen cock into Stacy, wishing she had a nice, round ass that he could smack and feel ripple up against his abs. He wanted to feel thick thighs wrapped around his waist as he pumped into her. But the thighs were too slender and what he felt wasn't what he imagined, because they didn't belong to the right woman.

She will have to do for now.

Pearson closed his eyes tight and imagined Monique's dark coffee eyes filled with pleasure that *he* had caused and he came with a long, low growl. *I have to have her.*

"Oh my gawd! Pear that was so awesome. What has gotten into you?" Stacy questioned, panting with wide indigo eyes.

"Don't call me that," Pearson snapped. He hated cutesy fucking nicknames. Stacy was just speeding up the remainder of her time she had left.

Stacy pouted her thin, pink lips he used to find so attractive, but now, they did nothing for him.

"Get in the shower. I'll call the driver to take you home." Pearson got up from the bed and slid on his boxer briefs before he stalked out of the room, leaving a pouting Stacy scrambling to the ensuite bathroom to do as she'd been told.

Pearson made his way down the stairs and into his home office. What he really wanted to do was have a large class of whiskey, but he tried to refrain from drinking during stressful times because he knew from experience that was how addiction began.

Pearson called for the driver before he logged onto his computer. The alerts went off like fireworks on the Fourth of July. He scanned the headlines, and a grunt of frustration left his mouth.

Tech Genius Degrades Women.

Pearson Grant Hates Female Reporters.

Pearson Grant's "Sorry" apology!

Pearson ran his hands through his hair and let out a deep, annoyed breath. *Fucking vultures! Monique was right. An apology wasn't good enough.*

He didn't want to hire a freaking image consultant of all people, but as she'd predicted, they were ripping him to shreds, and the show hadn't even aired yet. Pearson didn't want her help. Hell, he didn't want anybody's help, but it looked like he needed help.

Damn it!

"Pearson, I'm leaving. Aren't you going to walk me to the door?" Stacy had barged into his office still wearing a pout on her pretty face. The longer she stayed around pouting, the less attractive she became.

"No." His deep voice was emotionless. "I've never walked you to the door before. The car is waiting." Pearson heard her huff as she stomped out of his office.

Yeah, her time is done. Pearson logged off and headed to the shower. He had to get the smell of sex off of him, but he needed to wait for his "guest" to leave. She was becoming a stage-five clinger, and it was really starting to cramp his style, especially with the beautiful goddess plaguing his every thought, even during sex.

"Damn it, I need to get control," Pearson mumbled to himself as he let the hot water pour over his head. It was late, and he had a long day ahead of him. He had to deal with the unwanted help from a woman that he desperately craved.

PEARSON WAS DRESSED in a light blue single-breasted twill suit with a matching dress shirt. He wore a blue paisley pocket square with the top button of his shirt undone. A tie around his neck while he was so stressed felt like a noose, so he'd opted not to wear one today. He adjusted his silver cufflinks as he gazed out at the beautiful view outside his office.

"Grant, Ms. Carter is waiting in conference room one for you." Kelsey's voice came through loud and clear over the phone line.

"Thank you, Kelsey." Pearson gathered his things and headed to the conference room.

He had a sense of déjà vu, but this time, it wouldn't be an ambush. Pearson knew what he would be walking into. He knew that the woman he was trusting with his future was also the woman that held his every thought.

Pearson's stride was confident as he rounded the corner and faced the clear view of the conference room. He was anticipating another glimpse of his new obsession, but what he saw made his pulse quicken with fury.

Keifer was cozied up close to Monique. They looked to be in deep conversation and were smiling and laughing. Pearson felt an uncontrollable urge to punch Keifer in his smug-ass face then fire him. But he knew that his thoughts were crazy, so he reined in his temper and prepared himself for another day full of shit storms.

"Hi, Mr. Grant. We were just talking strategy." Monique's eyes were bright and hopeful.

"Well, the apology strategy didn't seem to work. They ripped me apart, saying it was insincere," Pearson grumbled, unable to stop himself from being negative. They were still sitting entirely too close together and it was raising all of his hackles. He took a seat as he scowled in their direction.

Pearson had never felt jealous or possessive about anyone before. But for some reason, Monique Carter had him feeling both, and he didn't know anything about the woman.

Well, I did online stalk her and requested an unofficial background check from my personal PI. But she hasn't told me anything about herself. That's what counts. Right?

"The apology worked like I said it would. We got mixed reviews, but for the most part, people believed what you said. You acknowledged that you said something wrong, you apologized, and you didn't make excuses. Believe me, that will go a long way," Monique stated passionately.

Pearson could tell she trusted what she was saying. He felt like a complete jackass, but he couldn't seem to stop himself. *Fucking Keifer is still sitting too close to her.*

"Mixed reviews aren't good enough, Ms. Carter. Do I need to remind you that both our reputations are on the line here?" Pearson narrowed his eyes when Keifer placed a comforting hand on Monique's shoulder.

Is he fucking kidding me? Why is he touching her so much?

"I'm not paying you two to play footsie while my image is continuously being tarnished. I pay you to fix *this*." Pearson pointed an accusatory finger at Monique. "And for you to make sure our marketing for Media Tech stays on track." He pointed at Keifer.

"If you two can't keep your hands off of each other long enough to do your jobs, then I can find replacements that can!" Pearson knew he was acting irrationally, but he couldn't stop himself. He was sure he looked like a man-child throwing a temper tantrum.

Control yourself, Grant. What are you, fucking twelve?

Pearson carefully put his blank mask back into place as he looked at the two objects of his ire. Keifer's eyebrows were raised in question and Monique looked like she was ready to spit fire at his head at any given moment.

Keifer cleared his throat, which after working with him for over thirteen years, Pearson knew it was a habit that Keifer executed whenever he was uncomfortable.

"We are hard at work, Pearson. Nobody is playing footsie. Monique's strategy *is* working. I just got a call today for an interview on a major network that will put that little syndicated show to shame."

"I'm not doing another fuck... listen no more interviews." Pearson tried to calm himself down again.

"Mr. Grant, Keifer is right. Your image hasn't been damaged any further at this point. We are both *professionals.* I take issue with you suggesting otherwise. I am here to do a job, and if you don't want to follow what I have to say per the contract we signed, then fine. I will take my money and leave. But I refuse to sit here and allow *you* to tarnish my reputation by suggesting I'm not doing what I was hired to do." Monique's expression was fierce, and her words, although harsh, had an undesirable effect on him. Pearson was hard as a rock.

Pearson subtly adjusted himself under the table, and hoped like hell neither of them noticed. He needed Monique's help whether he wanted to admit to it or not. And acting like an ass was just making it hard on both of them. For him, it made him actually hard.

Instead of apologizing like he should have, Pearson decided to steer the conversation back to fixing his problem.

"So if the apology sort of worked, then what are we going to do next besides more interviews? I'd rather not do another interview." Pearson wasn't shy nor did he lack confidence, but with his recent lack of control he, was deathly afraid that he would go off on another rant if he was provoked. Neither he nor his company could afford that.

Monique stared for a moment as though she was making some sort of decision. Pearson wished he knew what she was thinking.

"Okay. No interviews for the time being. But at some point, you *will* have to do one." Monique gave him a stern look before continuing. "I will make sure that the environment is controlled and you are prepared for the questions. But we will get you media training before any of that happens. And *that* is a nonnegotiable."

Of course, Pearson didn't think that he needed any kind of training, but he wouldn't rock the boat right now. He would just keep putting it off until Monique relinquished.

"Okay. No interviews for now. So what's next?" Pearson asked, glazing over the rest of the deal.

"We need to discuss your *personal life*." Pearson watched Monique glance over at Keifer with a worried expression.

Shit.

"Alright, what about my personal life?" Pearson questioned, trying to remain calm.

"I have spoken to some ladies about your relationships."

"Why?" Pearson sat up, trying not to glare at Monique or Keifer. He knew that his public life had an effect on his image and his company. But he was very careful about his personal life. Pearson took extra precautions to make sure his private life stayed private.

"I had to make sure there wasn't anything in your past that anyone could use against you. We already have one recording, so I wanted to make sure we didn't have any random porn stars that were going to pop up to sue you." Monique smirked and Pearson wanted to be annoyed, but she was too sexy to even make him feel irritated.

"No porn stars." Pearson smirked back. "I'm a grown man. I have relationships. I make sure everything is consensual and nobody is married. When a relationship is over, I don't look back."

Pearson watched Monique purse her lips, but she nodded.

"That was the general consensus. However, if you have any relationship skeletons in your closet, I need to know."

"No skeletons either," Pearson responded without thought.

"Are you sure? Because we need to release any information before the press does," Monique insisted her face tense.

"As much as I hate it, I'm an open book *for you*. I don't have anything to hide."

"Great! Now that that's out of the way, let's discuss this charity event that you need to attend on Saturday. You should bring a date," Keifer added unwelcomed, entering the conversation.

Pearson glared at Keifer. He didn't know what Keifer was playing at, but Pearson never brought dates to anything. And he'd be damned if he would bring a date to some God-forsaken charity event that he didn't want to attend in the first place.

"I don't think it's necessary for me to bring a date. As bad as you two seem to think my reputation is, I've never been accused of being a womanizer."

"That's one more thing I can cross off my list," Monique mumbled, but Pearson still heard her.

"So tomorrow is Friday. I will be at my office, and you will be preparing for the event on Saturday. There will be press in attendance. However, it is a very big political event, so you shouldn't be the focus," Monique stated.

"What is this event and how long will I have to stay?" Pearson questioned, his annoyance back at the idea of a wasted Saturday night.

"It's a STEM for girls' event," Monique answered.

"Science, technology, engineering, and math," Keifer cut in unnecessarily to explain the acronym.

"I own a tech company. I know what STEM means." Pearson scoffed.

"Anyway..." Monique sighed. "You're going to give an incredibly large amount of money and you're going to stay away from the press."

This is costing me more than my image.

5

OFF TRACK

Monique should've been disappointed that her weekend plans with Damon had to be changed once again. However, she was relieved that she wouldn't have to spend the night focusing on all of the things that were wrong with their relationship. Instead, they would have a date night wearing elegant clothes and doing good for a charitable organization.

It was Thursday night and Monique had had a successful day. Pearson wasn't a push over, but at least he had somewhat given in to her demands. It was a win in her book, so Monique decided to call her friend, Nikki, to see if she wanted to meet her for drinks.

Nicole Hutson, who went by the nickname Nikki, was an ex-coworker turned good friend. The two women often hung out or networked together. Monique and Nikki used to work together at Bedford and Stein. It was the PR firm that Monique had left to start her own company. Nikki was still there grinding away as a junior executive.

"Well, damn! She *is* alive. I thought you had moved to another country or something." Nikki had answered her phone on the second ring.

"I know, lady. I'm sorry. I have been so busy lately," Monique explained.

"Oh yeah? So your *little* business keeps you that busy, huh?" Nikki questioned in a tone that Monique didn't recognize from her friend.

Monique had a feeling that Nikki was more than a little upset that she had blown her off one too many times to hang out with Damon or to work. Monique felt guilty for neglecting her friend, so she didn't address the little shade Nikki had thrown at her.

"I do alright. Listen, why don't you meet me out for drinks so we can catch up? My treat." Monique quickly changed the subject to something happier. She wanted to celebrate, not get into some petty argument with her friend.

"You're treating? Okay, big baller. Who's going?" Nikki questioned tentatively.

"Just me and you, if you can make it."

"What? You didn't invite Venus? She's your ride or die." Monique could hear the smile in Nikki's voice and she knew she was teasing her.

Everyone said that Monique and Venus were two peas in a pod. Wherever you found one, you would find the other. It had been that way since high school and it wasn't about to change.

"V is away for work, so it will just be the two of us," Monique said, smiling.

"Cool. Where do you want to go?"

The friends ironed out the details of their impromptu girls' night out, and Monique headed home to freshen up. She would need to make a call to Damon to see if he could go with her to the charity event on Saturday and call her mother to cancel for Sunday dinner.

Nah, I'll just text Mama. She'll nag me to death if I call.

Once Monique made it home, she ended up texting both Damon and her mom. Damon confirmed that he could take her out Saturday and he would call her later. Her mom didn't respond.

It took another hour for Monique to shower, reapply her makeup, and change into something girls' night out worthy. With her busy schedule, it wasn't often that she got to hang out with just her friends, even if it was just two of them tonight. She was just touching up her lip gloss and heading for the door when her phone rang.

"Hello?"

"Hey, babe. I thought I would drop by tonight so we could properly make up." Damon was using his bedroom voice, but Monique couldn't even pretend to get aroused. They really needed to fix what was going on between them. *Just not tonight.*

"Sorry, D. You must've missed my text; I'm meeting up with Nikki. I was just on my way out."

"*Nikki?* I thought ya'll didn't talk anymore."

"No. What gave you that idea?" Monique asked, confused.

"Nothing. Nothing. I just haven't heard you talk about her or hang out with her lately. That's all."

"Oh. Well, that's because we've both been busy lately. That's why we're going out, so we can catch up," Monique answered happily.

"Okay, honey. Have fun with your friend and don't stay out too late. And text me when you make it home." Damon actually sounded like the boyfriend he used to be. It was a welcomed surprise.

Monique had prepared herself for another argument. Damon normally hated when she went out with her friends.

"Alright, babe. I'll text you as soon as I'm home. Talk to ya later." Monique's day just seemed to be getting better and better.

Monique met Nikki in a spot not too far from her place. It was a quaint little bar and lounge called Evolve. The R & B was bumping throughout the space, and the crowd consisted of well-dressed young professionals. Monique hadn't realized how popular the spot had become.

She made her way through the door and spotted Nikki at the bar chatting with a tall handsome Latino man. As Monique approached, the two seemed to be wrapping up their conversation. The man caressed Nikki's cheek and kissed her on the lips before he backed away. As he turned to leave, he gave Monique a slow perusal before sending a wink in her direction.

The hell? Monique frowned at the man and shook her head.

Dogs everywhere.

"Hey, girl!" the two women greeted each other.

They gave hugs and air kisses before Monique settled in beside Nikki on an empty barstool. The callous man forgotten, they ordered drinks and let the vibe of the atmosphere relax them.

"So, how's work going? Is B & S still treating you well?" Monique questioned as she sipped her drink.

"Why? Are you doing so well with your little start-up that you can pay me a bigger salary?" Nikki smiled, but that was the second time she had made a dig at Monique's business.

Monique arched a brow in wonder. *Is she mad that I moved on?*

"My company is growing, but no, I can't afford you." Monique laughed off Nikki's comment. "But I'm working with a big client now, so maybe soon, I could offer you something."

Nikki sat up and smiled mischievously. "I knew something was going on. You never want to just come out. So this new client must be a *man*, huh? 'Cause you have been smiling and glowing since you walked in."

"What? No. It's nothing like that." Monique waved her friend off. "I just made a lot of progress with a difficult client. Besides, I would never do anything like that to Damon."

"That on-again, off-again mess with Damon is nothing to be loyal to. You need to loosen up and have a little fun," Nikki replied dismissively.

"On again, off again?" Monique was confused. "We've never broken up. We have our little arguments, but…"

Monique was defending the very relationship she thought about ending for good. But with all their faults, they hadn't broken up. *But we are on again, off again, even if we don't officially break up.* Monique was lost in thought for a minute before Nikki's voice brought her back to reality.

"I didn't mean anything. If you want to be with Damon, that's none of my business. I just think that anybody that has you wanting to have fun is somebody you should consider keeping around."

Monique just shook her head at her friend. She wasn't sure what Nikki was fishing for, but cheating was not her style. Pearson

Grant was her client, and as fine as he was, she would never cross that line.

After a few more drinks, the conversation got lighter, and the two women fell into a familiar comfort. The ambiance was chill, the music was pumping, and the laughter was flowing. And before they knew it, two hours had passed.

"Girl, isn't that your sister over there talking to that fine-ass dude?" Nikki asked, looking over Monique's shoulder.

Monique hated to even look. But she did, and that's when she locked eyes with her sister. *Damn! I knew my day was going too well.*

Monique watched the scowl grow on her sister's pretty face. Before long, the other woman sashayed in her direction. It was a mystery to Monique that she and her sister could be at such odds. Although they'd bickered growing up like normal siblings, their relationship now was nonexistent. They couldn't even be in the same room together for more than fifteen minutes before the arguing started. The sad part about it all was that Monique didn't understand where the animosity was coming from. A lot of things happened when they were younger, but it'd had nothing to do with Monique.

Their mom constantly babied Ashley, and although it annoyed Monique sometimes, she wasn't mad at her sister about it. Monique had every reason to be upset at their mom, though, because no matter what she did or how successful she was, Luanne Carter always had to criticize her eldest child. However, Monique still wasn't mad. She loved and respected her mother, and even though their mother could work her nerves like nobody else and she'd made a lot of mistakes when raising them, Monique still wasn't angry with her. She wanted a better relationship with her sister, but it didn't seem like Ashley wanted the same.

"I'm surprised to see you out, especially with..." Ashley sneered at Nikki. "...*her*. I'm surprised you're not sitting up under Damon somewhere."

"Hey, Ash, nice to see you too," Monique stated sarcastically before sipping on her glass of wine that she now wished was a shot of whiskey.

Ashley frowned as she narrowed her eyes. Monique just wanted a relaxing, fun evening with her friend. *Why Lord? Why must I deal with the devil constantly?*

"Moni, I'm going to the restroom. I'll be back." Nikki slid off her seat and walked away without acknowledging Ashley. Monique wished she could follow her so she wouldn't have to stay and finish this awkward-ass conversation with her sister. The last time they were in the same room, Monique had threatened to beat her up.

"Okay, girl," Monique finally responded to Nikki.

Ashley took the seat Nikki vacated. She was still frowning, and Monique knew that she was looking for a fight.

"You need better friends," Ashley said, looking at Nikki's retreating back in disgust.

I need a better sister, Monique thought, but responded, "You don't even know that woman."

"I know enough," Ashley responded cryptically.

Monique rolled her eyes. "Did you come over here just to be petty or..." Monique let her words trail off.

"You think you're so smart. Ain't nobody being petty. You just don't ever want to listen to nobody," Ashley responded with her face still scrunched up. She looked like she'd been eating lemons while smelling something nasty.

"Girl! What do you want? I was having a nice time, and then here you come. You can't just speak and go on and live your life?" Monique was so tired of her damn sister.

"See? That's what's wrong with you—"

"What's wrong with me is that my very own sister can't stand to see me happy and enjoying myself. Every time I have something good, you want to ruin it. Whatever it is that I did to you, I. Am. Sorry. But you got to let me live, sis. Your funky attitude every time we see each other is exhausting. If you can't let whatever your problem is go, then you need to either smile and nod or ignore my ass altogether. Because from now on, that's what I'm going to do to you."

Monique signaled for the bartender. She slipped a couple of bills in his hand and walked away. She pulled out her phone and sent

Nikki a text that she was going to her car. She would wait to see if her friend wanted to go somewhere else before she headed home. But before she could get to the door she heard her name being called.

"Moni, girl, are you leaving?" Nikki asked, coming toward her.

"I just sent you a text. Do you want to go somewhere else? I invited you out and it's still early, but my sister has gotten on my nerves."

Nikki chuckled. "I'm glad you said it. No, we don't have to go anywhere else. I have an early morning tomorrow."

The ladies exchanged hugs and they parted ways after making plans to catch up later. Monique decided to send Damon a text, but when he didn't respond, she just figured he was busy. *Oh well, I will just have to relax at home.*

To Monique's surprise, when she got home, Damon was waiting for her with flowers. She felt a little guilty for thinking he was trying to ghost her again when he didn't respond to her text.

"Ms. Carter, these are for you." Damon handed her the collection of wild flowers.

"Thank you, D. This is so sweet of you." Monique smiled and kissed his lips softly.

Damon smiled, flashing those deep dimples. His light brown complexion turned red, and his dark eyes shined at the compliment.

Damon Hicks was everything Monique wanted in a man. He was the epitome of tall, dark, and handsome. Damon had dark chocolate eyes, and a smile that wouldn't quit. He wore his hair in tiny locs that hung down past his shoulders. He often pulled them back out of his face. He worked as an engineer and he was one of the smartest people Monique knew.

When they first met, he was attentive, loving, and sweet. He was always doing little things for her like buying flowers for no reason or popping up to bring her lunch when he knew she wouldn't have time to eat. He understood how busy she was and he never held that against her.

Damon never complained or nagged about her working too much. He just gave her the love and support she needed. Monique thought at this point in their relationship they should be headed toward marriage, but it looked like they were taking steps backwards.

For the past year, Damon had been hinting around about living together. However, Monique made it clear that there would be no shacking up no matter how good of a man he was. *Why buy the cow?* Her mother would throw a fit, and she agreed that she didn't want to play wifey. If he was serious, then a ring had to be on her finger before they made a move.

When Monique didn't give in to his constant badgering, he slowly started to pull away. And for the last couple of months he had been MIA every weekend. Monique was afraid that he may have been cheating, but as strong as she was, she wasn't ready to face the fact that another one of her relationships had failed.

Damon's strong masculine scent brought Monique out of her morose thoughts and back to the hopeful-looking present. Damon had wrapped his arms around her waist as she unlocked her front door.

Once they were inside with the door shut behind them, Damon leaned down and kissed her lips with passion he hadn't displayed in a while. Monique ate up the attention as his firm lips took over the kiss. She opened her mouth and let his tongue run over hers.

They tugged at one another's clothes as they made their way to her bedroom. They kissed and caressed until they fell onto her king-sized bed naked. Their touching was frantic almost to the point of desperation, but something felt off.

No! Monique, keep your head in the game. Reconnect and get back on track with your man.

Monique ran her hands down Damon's muscled abdomen. His six-foot body lay underneath hers like a stallion ready to be ridden. She slid her wet sex over his long, hard dick, working herself up to the edge of climax.

"Stop playing and put it in," Damon growled deeply.

"Condom first." Monique leaned over to her nightstand and pulled one from their stash and ripped it open.

Damon grunted his frustration. Condoms were another point of contention in their relationship. Damon didn't want to wear them, but Monique insisted they would until they were ready for a bigger commitment. So his frustration didn't stop Monique from sliding the latex down his rigid member before she slipped it inside of her.

Monique moaned as she began to ride him. The tension built up in her again as she moved up and down. The friction on her clit from her movements was sending her straight to ecstasy.

"Yeah! Ride that shit! Fuck me, Monique," Damon moaned as he sat up. He moved his strong hands to her hips and began to pound her from underneath. He sucked on her nipples as his hands moved to almost painfully grip her ass.

Damon's hand moved from her ass to her belly. He leaned back and placed his large thumb on her clit. He rubbed frantic circles around her nub until Monique's eyes rolled to the back of her head.

"Ummm! Damn! That feels so good!" Monique shouted as her climax sent her body into waves of elation.

Damon followed her over the edge with a long drawn-out groan. As Monique moved from on top of Damon to her side of the bed, both of them lay panting, coming down from their sexual high. Once her breathing was under control, she rolled over to snuggle with Damon. Instead of him cuddling her, he moved to get out of the bed.

"I have an early morning, so I'm gonna head out." Damon hastily began moving toward the bathroom and once inside, he shut the door behind him.

"Really?" Monique sat up and hollered at the closed door.

"So much for getting back on track," Monique mumbled to herself as she flopped down on her bed in frustration.

6

SETBACKS

Pearson hated socializing, especially at stuffy charity events. Usually, Mark, his VP, did all of the necessary schmoozing so Pearson wouldn't have to. But Pearson had to admit that after some research about the program, he was actually looking forward to the STEM banquet the next night. As a matter of fact, Monique had sent over a schedule of events he needed to attend, and Pearson had an interest in all of them. The STEM was an obvious choice because of the technology, but the ALS golf event touched him.

Ten years' prior, Pearson's mother had passed away from the horrible debilitating disease, and finding both treatment and a cure was something Pearson always wanted to contribute to, but never got the chance. Until Monique.

With all the focus on him for the past week, Pearson's meetings concerning his company had been pushed back. He hated that his business continued to suffer because of his off-the-cuff remarks. Although he apologized, he still felt ashamed that he had allowed the woman to push him out of character. *You have to stay in control.*

Pearson sighed. He couldn't change the past or what he thought about that ignorant reporter. He was a thirty-seven-year-old man who had to learn to do better.

As Pearson sat through another meeting about software bugs on the company's latest app, his notifications beeped. Anytime his named was mentioned on a blog or became a trending topic, a notification was automatically sent to him. The last thing he felt like doing after a day full of meetings was seeing something else that may set his already frayed nerves on end, but he didn't have a choice.

Monique wanted to make sure he was kept up to speed on everything that was being said and everything that was happening concerning his reputation. Pearson didn't feel it was necessary for him to see every single thing anybody had to say, but she insisted it was important that he stay in the loop. So once the meeting was over, he headed to his office to sift through the notifications.

Pearson couldn't believe his eyes as he read the article in the *Dallas Daily*.

Darlene Austin of the Wake Up With Us Morning Show explains how Mr. Pearson Grant made her feel with his demeaning remarks about her appearance. "I would like to think in this day and age, a man wouldn't feel so comfortable body shaming a woman."

"Body shaming! What the fuck!" Pearson bellowed.

"Kelsey!" Pearson yelled for his assistant. "Get Monique Carter here *now*!"

"I can't believe I apologized to that woman!" Pearson paced back and forth in front of his desk. "She knows damn well her ass and tits are fake! How the hell is that body shaming?"

He was beyond livid. It was obvious that Darlene was going to milk this situation for all it was worth. There was no way in hell that Pearson could let some fame chaser ruin everything that he worked for.

Ten minutes later, Keifer walked into the office with a calm-looking Monique following. The two of them walking in together, served to piss him off even more.

"I shouldn't have to call you," Pearson ranted at Monique. "Your whole plan is crumbling around us, and *I* had to call you."

"You didn't *have* to call me, Mr. Grant. Your assistant should've let you know that I was already on my way when she called," Monique stated still with a calm that made Pearson want to spit fire.

"Pearson, Monique has a contingency plan for this. You need to calm down." Keifer placed his hand on the small of Monique's back and pulled out a chair for her to sit down.

Pearson could only see red. Keifer was entirely too fucking comfortable.

"Why are you here? Telling me to calm down in my own damn office! I didn't call for you? You are in charge of the marketing for the company. The last time I checked the stocks, we were doing fine," Pearson addressed Keifer sharply.

Keifer's eyebrows raised high on his forehead. Pearson read the shock that was written all over his face, but his possessive nature wouldn't let Keifer's familiarity with Monique slide. Pearson knew that he had bigger things to worry about, but he couldn't get the image of Keifer's hands on Monique out of his mind.

"I am the head of the marketing and public relations department of this firm. I have been since you started Media Tech Innovation. Remember me," Keifer pointed to himself. "Longtime friend. I'm here because you need my help. And obviously, you have lost your damn mind at some point."

Pearson rubbed his hands down his face with irritation. He knew he was wrong, but he refused to apologize for his behavior. Apologizing was what had gotten him into this shit in the first place.

Actually, your derogatory words got you into this, Pearson's conscience taunted.

"Okay, gentlemen, we have a lot of work to do, so I need you both to focus," Monique chimed in with a look of exasperation.

"I have done my research on Ms. Austin. I didn't think that she would be so eager to release a statement before her own show, but it looked like your apology worked. And now, she's scrambling to keep the story relevant for sweeps."

"This is your last chance at a strategy. I don't want to be blind-sided by any more of this bullshit. I have a company to run. If my image is already shit, and you can't rectify this situation, then I will take the hit and make sure Media Tech Innovation's products continue to be stellar so it can remain successful."

"Pearson, you know if it was that easy, we wouldn't even bother to try to fix your image. The CEO's reputation will have a direct effect on the company whether you like it or not. Monique *can* fix this. You just have to trust her."

Even though Pearson didn't appreciate Keifer's two cents, essentially, he was right. Pearson knew that, but his uncontrollable urges of possession around Monique were getting out of hand and he needed to put some distance between them.

However, if he couldn't fire her and put them at a physical distance, maybe being a dick would place a wall of resistance around his irrational behavior toward a woman that he barely even knew.

"This is no longer a strategy. This is your new way of life. I have a media expert coming in today. He will work with you on spontaneous interview questions. No comment will not work after today's shenanigans. At tomorrow's event, you will be asked about this and you are going to reach deep down in your soul, so you can appear charming."

Keifer snickered, and if Pearson wasn't still fuming, he would've laughed as well. He had been called a lot of names in his life, but *charming* definitely wasn't one of them.

"You have been accused of body shaming," Monique reminded him.

"That is beyond ridiculous," Pearson cut in.

"Yeah, they absolutely took that out of context. However, it's already out there. So until we show them otherwise, you will be the big bad wolf in this scenario."

Monique's smooth words and melodic voice made Pearson want to be the big bad wolf. He was absolutely ready and willing to lure her to bed and eat all her goodies.

"So we will make sure he will do that." Keifer's annoying voice broke into Pearson's midday fantasy.

"What will you make sure I will do?" Pearson questioned, confused as hell that Keifer thought he could just tell him what to do.

"You need to focus, man. Come on," Keifer responded with a mischievous look on his face.

"You need a date to the event tomorrow." Pearson tried to cut in again, but Monique held up her delicate hand to keep him quiet. "I get that you don't want to and before it would've been fine. But you need a date that will help with your credibility, someone that is both pretty and smart. Not a model, though. It will just fuel the fire that you're a pig."

"So I'll take *you* then." Pearson smiled at his own idea. This was the perfect way to get to know her better.

"*M-me*? No. You can't take me to an event. All someone would do is put it together that I am a specialist and figure out that you're a client. That's not how I do things."

"So? Why would it matter? It's more than obvious I need help. I think it would be a smart move to take someone like you." Pearson smiled.

He thought Monique would be flattered, but a frown appeared on her beautiful face, and he hated that he was the one who'd put it there.

"What do you mean someone like me?" Monique's eyebrow arched in question and her gorgeous, plump lips were held in a sexy pout.

Damn, that's sexy.

"Not my usual type," Pearson answered slowly.

"I know I'm not a model," Monique stated sharply, her professionalism slipping slightly.

"No, I mean you're intelligent, you own a successful business, and you're absolutely stunning." Pearson smiled at the shy look Monique gave him.

"Thank you, Pearson." Monique smiled and if he wasn't mistaken, she was blushing.

"You are so welcome." Pearson couldn't help but flirt, and he noticed she'd finally called him by his first name.

"But I can't be your date. I have a boyfriend and I wouldn't want to give any ammunition against you. The press can turn a friendly outing into a torrid affair. But I'll tell you what, why don't you skip the red carpet for this event, and we will work on getting you a suitable date for future events."

Pearson wanted to demand to know who the hell this guy was and why his PI hadn't gotten back to him with this information. He wanted to punch the hell out of whoever this man was, and make Monique go with him to the benefit.

But instead of being a total psycho that threw tantrums and showed how unstable he could be, Pearson decided to focus all of his energy on getting to know who Monique Carter was. Then he would be able to catch his prey.

"I don't mind going by myself. It's what I wanted anyway." Pearson tried to smile, but he knew that he looked like a predator baring his teeth, because that's exactly what he was.

THE REST of Friday afternoon was spent with Pearson in company meetings, and Keifer and Monique planning their next move. Although his actions would say differently, Pearson trusted both of them to do what was necessary to get him out of this mess.

Since Darlene's article had come out, Pearson was once again at the top of the trending topic list. Monique was cool as a cucumber. She told him they would stop focusing on Darlene Austin and start focusing on changing the narrative on who Pearson was.

So in order to shift the focus to the positive, Pearson Grant, the worst asshole of all the assholes collectively, was now standing in a tuxedo on a Saturday night, laughing and talking to a group of ten-year-old girls about a robot they had built. The conversation was so intriguing to him that he didn't even realize that he was no longer focused on his reputation. Pearson was genuinely enjoying himself at a charity event. *Who'd a thought?*

Pearson was in the midst of a full belly laugh at two girls who were exchanging sassy retorts on the obvious need of black girl magic in the field of technology when like a beaming moon in the middle of a darken sky, all of his attention was stolen.

As soon as he could, he excused himself from the conversation. It was like her silver dress was beckoning him. The metallic sheen of the material flowed like liquid around her curves. And then... she smiled. Pearson would've thought his heart stopped if it wasn't pounding so loudly in his ears. His feet were moving without his permission, and before he knew it, he was standing in front of her.

She looked magnificent. Her hair was cascading to one side, accenting the natural definition of her cheekbones. Her bright eyes were more pronounced under sparkly eye shadow and long dark lashes. Pearson was absolutely blown away.

"Mr. Grant, it looks like you are having a good time." Monique smiled up at him, her pink stained lips growing wide over perfect white teeth.

Pearson wanted to frown at the formal use of his name, but instead, he nodded and gave her a small smirk.

"Yes, I actually am, *Monique.*" He quirked an eyebrow at her and he was fairly certain she was blushing once again.

"Hi, Pearson Grant. Nice to finally meet you," the man beside Monique greeted. Pearson barely noticed the man standing there. "I'm Damon Hicks, Monique's boyfriend."

Pearson shook the other man's hand without ceremony. However, Pearson had observed him enough. Like him, the other man was dressed in a black tuxedo. His dreads were pulled neatly back into a ponytail. He stood proudly beside Monique, but his eyes were narrowed and he looked like he wanted to pummel Pearson for daring to speak to her. *Yeah, buddy the feeling is mutual.*

"So, you're the secret boyfriend." Pearson smirked at Damon. His dark eyes were now mere slits of fury gazing in Pearson's direction.

"*Secret*?" Damon turned his glare toward Monique, and Pearson had to stop himself from stepping between them.

"It's not a secret just because you didn't know, Pearson." Monique rolled her eyes, and Pearson smiled. *Back to first names.*

"True." Pearson chuckled. "But to be fair, all of our attention was centered on me."

"Right. But she does *work* for you." Damon had put so much stress on the word work that Pearson got the impression that Damon didn't like the idea.

Pearson watched as Monique squinted at her boyfriend, her mouth held in a thin line. *Interesting.*

"Well, as many hoops that I have to jump through at her say so, I would say that was the other way around," Pearson responded as the tension between the three climbed.

"Hmmm," Damon hummed, but his eyes stayed narrowed at Monique.

Before the conversation could become even more awkward, the pings of Pearson and Monique's cell phones grabbed their attention.

Pearson was amazed what he was looking at. It was a picture of him laughing and talking with the girls from the STEM program not even twenty minutes before. The headline read, *Pearson Grant Gives Back.* The article was super short, but it was positive.

"How the hell did they get this up so fast?" Pearson questioned Monique, looking around the room.

"I called in a couple of favors. They're just quicker than even I'd expected. But my favors aren't the only ones here, so stay on your P's and Q's because they're definitely watching." Monique smiled brightly.

"You got it, boss lady." Pearson winked.

Before Monique could reply, a husky voice interrupted their conversation.

"Hello, dear sister. I didn't know that you were going to be here tonight."

"Ashley? What are you doing here?" Monique replied.

And just like that the tension in the air was back up to a thousand degrees.

7

IT WAS ALL A LIE

My sister keeps popping up like the clown in the IT movie, *heffah what do you want?* Monique knew that her face was reflecting her thoughts because Pearson's bright eyes were assessing her closely with a look of confusion on his handsome face. Even Damon's look of contempt had softened toward her with the appearance of her sister.

"I'm here with my date, Cedrick. He works for the STEM program. Now, what are *you* doing here?" Ashley was talking to Monique, but her eyes kept darting between Damon and Pearson.

"I invited her," Pearson spoke up. "I'm Pearson Grant," Pearson introduced himself saving Monique from having to answer.

"I'm Ashley Carter, Monique's younger sister." Ashley held out her hand, and Pearson brought it to his lips to kiss the back of it.

Monique tensed at the intimate contact between the two. She didn't understand why she felt uncomfortable, so she stepped closer to Damon for support. He smiled down at her, and squeezed her hand.

"Oh, Monique you didn't tell me you had such a beautiful sister," Pearson commented as he smiled widely at Ashley.

"Monique doesn't really like to talk about me." Ashley smirked.

Monique didn't know what sin she had committed for God to constantly punish her with her sister's presence, but she would make sure to grovel on her knees for forgiveness. She'd seen Ashley more in the past week than she had in the last four months, and each time was worse.

"Hi, D. You doin' alright?" Ashley turned her smirk towards Damon and batted her lashes.

Damon cleared his throat uncomfortably. "I'm good."

Monique knew the score this time. Ashley's little baiting game wouldn't work. They were at a charity gala for kids, wearing pretty dresses and sipping champagne. There was no way in hell that Monique was about to argue with her sister.

The tension was thick, and Monique knew that if the paparazzi were taking pictures at this moment, it would show all over their faces. Monique took a deep breath, relaxed, and pasted on a smile. This was her career on the line. Pearson needed her to make over his image, not have him in the middle of some family feud.

"Ash, sweetheart." A stocky built black man with milk chocolate skin and onyx colored eyes walked up, and put his arm possessively around Ashley's waist.

Monique noticed the smile on her sister's face, and it made her pause. At that moment, she wished that they had a closer relationship, one where they shared each other's lives and were happy for one another.

"I'm Cedrick Watson." The men shook hands and he greeted Monique with a smile and a small hand shake as well.

After introductions were made, small talk continued a little uncomfortably until dinner was announced and they separated to go to their tables.

Monique was glad that there were assigned seats and Ashley was sitting with her date and not at the same table with them. Damon had gone eerily quiet, and Pearson was engaged in conversation with the other couples seated with them. Monique periodically checked her phone and she was glad to see that there weren't any negative updates about Pearson.

As the dinner droned on, Damon excused himself from the table. Coincidentally, the tension left with him. As soon as he was gone, Pearson turned his attention toward Monique.

"You seem a little tense. Everything okay?" he questioned. Monique could see the curiosity written all over his handsome face, but her problems were her own. There was no way she was sharing her troubles with her client. *I'm the fixer, damn it! I don't have problems.*

Monique knew that she had to suck it up and be professional. Although it seemed like all of her personal problems were in the same room, she refused to address anything while she was in front of her client. Her strategy was working, and she would put all her energy into making sure she was successful at least in business.

"Everything is fine." She gave Pearson her professional smile, and he gave her a little frown. *What was that?*

"If you say so." He continued to stare at her, and Monique squirmed in her chair guiltily.

Pearson Grant made her feel things that she wasn't comfortable feeling about someone other than her boyfriend. Monique was all out of sorts, and she had to focus on getting herself together. *As soon as this situation is handled. I'm going to work on me.*

Before Monique could answer, Pearson's eyes narrowed at something behind her, and he excused himself from the table. Damon still hadn't returned, and the other couples were occupied with one another. Monique sat quietly, observing the spacious event and the other patrons.

It was a virtual who's who in the technology field as well as local politics. The Dallas mayor as well as the police chief were in attendance. Monique was glad that Pearson had been photographed with the children who were there instead of some of the political figures.

In a situation as fragile as Pearson's, it was better for him to keep any political affiliations to a minimum. The political climate in today's society was unstable, most of the public viewed politicians as entitled assholes, and they were trying to get Pearson out of that category.

The dinner was wrapping up, and the results of the silent auction were about to be announced when Damon finally returned. He had been acting peculiar all evening, but Monique didn't want to bring it up until they were alone.

"You alright?" Monique questioned, her eyes roaming over her boyfriend's disheveled appearance. His tie was slightly skewed, and a few of his dreads had escaped his once neat ponytail.

"I'm fine." He cleared his throat nervously as he straightened his tie.

"You sure? 'Cause it looks like you got into a fight." Monique went to tuck his hair back in the band and Damon caught her hand roughly.

Monique snatched her hand away confused. "What's wrong with you?" she whispered angrily.

"Monique, are you okay?" Pearson's deep voice sent shivers down her spine, but she refused to address her body's reaction. She took a deep breath trying to get herself together.

"I'm great," she answered overly cheerful, and winced at her own voice. She placed a faux smile on her face and turned to Damon. "We were going to head out. I was just waiting for you, so I could let you know we were leaving. The auction shouldn't take long. Do you think you can handle yourself without me?" She tried to sound nonchalant, but with the grim look on Pearson's face, she knew that her tone conveyed the uneasiness instead of the calm she was going for.

"I'll be fine. I was actually about to head out myself. I've had enough excitement for one night," Pearson replied cryptically. Monique shrugged. Their mission had been accomplished. Pearson was seen doing a good deed and nothing inappropriate had happened. All and all it was a successful night. However, Monique still felt like she was missing something.

It had been almost a week since the charity event, and Monique had been drenched in work. Along with Pearson, she had several small clients that were being handled. She wanted to make sure that all of her clients were happy with her service.

There were a few snippets of Pearson's interview put out to promote the upcoming show, but the frenzy was dying down just like Monique had predicted it would. It had only been two weeks, and the public had already started to forget.

Everything in her professional life was going according to plan. However, her personal life was suffering more and more with each passing day. After the charity event, Damon seemed to grow increasingly irritated at the mention of her business.

Monique gave all of her free time to Damon, and he still wasn't satisfied. He was unreasonable about her spending time with Nikki and Venus and he didn't even want her to go to Sunday dinner at her mother's.

With things finally calming down at work, Monique decided that it was time to address the elephant in the room. There was a reason Damon had been acting irrational, and it was time for her to find out what it was. Monique was tired of trying to please a man who acted as if her feelings didn't matter. Her relationship with Damon was hard work, and love isn't supposed to be hard.

Monique sat on her couch waiting for Damon to arrive. He was already an hour late, which served to piss her off. He had badgered her all day at work, calling and texting, but as soon as she was home alone and ready to talk, he was MIA. She didn't have any idea how an engineer had so much time during the day to call his girlfriend, especially since he didn't seem to have the time in the past.

When her cell beeped with a text, Monique sighed. She knew that Damon was avoiding her again. But this time, she wouldn't just sit and wait for him to come and apologize. There was no reason for his behavior. It was time for her to put on her big girl panties and face the truth. It was over between the two of them, and no matter how much she wished it wasn't, it was.

Monique thought about what she wanted to do, and she decided that she needed her best friend's advice to make it through. There was one thing she could count on with Venus Smith, and that was honesty.

Venus answered her phone after just one ring. "Hey, girl, what's going on? I was just about to call you."

Monique smiled. They always seemed to know when the other was in need.

"I need to break up with Damon, and his ass is ghosting me," Monique replied.

Venus chuckled. "Are you breaking up, breaking up or are you just trying to get him to lay down the good dick to get you to stay because we both know how ya'll two do things."

Monique wanted to be upset, but she knew her friend was right. They were stuck doing this dance, and she was officially done with it. Monique knew that it was time to fix herself.

"I'm done. I'm pretty sure he's cheating, and I just don't want to keep going on like this. I'm not in love with him anymore, and it's unfair to him. So I need to just let this shit go."

Venus sighed loudly. "I'm glad you finally woke your ass up. It was exhausting watching you two do the same mess over and over again."

"Nikki said the same thing. Was it really that obvious?" Monique questioned.

"First of all, I'm surprised Nikki said anything worth a damn, especially if it wasn't about herself. But I can admit the bitch was right," Venus replied dryly.

Monique chuckled. "Yeah, I guess everybody was right."

"Listen. Don't go beating yourself up. I know how you are. Being the fixer for everyone but yourself. But you deserve happiness, and if Damon doesn't make you happy, cut that dude loose and move on. If he's cheating and you're sad, let it go, sis."

Monique knew that Venus was right, and it was time that she fixed what was broken.

"Thanks, sister-friend. I knew that I could count on you. I'm going to go fix this mess, I'll call you crying later," Monique said jokingly. But she knew if she really did need to cry, Venus would be there in a heartbeat.

"Okay. Love you, sister-friend. Be the strong woman that I know you are."

"Love you too. And I will. I promise." Monique disconnected the call and headed toward the door. She was going straight to Damon's while she still had her nerve.

Monique practiced what she would say to Damon all the way to his house. Two years was a long time to invest in a relationship, and she didn't take walking away lightly. But staying with someone for the sake of time was stupid. Just because you were with someone for a long time, it didn't mean you should stay with them, especially if you were unhappy.

When Monique pulled up to Damon's house, she couldn't say that she was surprised to see him kissing another woman intimately. His hands were gripping her round ass like it was his lifeline. Her hands were tugging at his dreads as she grinded against him.

In her mind's eye, Monique saw herself jumping out of the car and dragging the woman by her hair away from Damon. She would lay her ass out with one punch and then turn her fury toward the cheating son of a bitch that called himself her man.

Monique could see herself beating the hell out of both of them. How dare they disrespect her? She was a good woman. She was hard-working, loving, owned her own shit, and intelligent. Why the hell would anybody want to cheat on her?

She wanted to fight, scream, and cuss. But she wouldn't. Damon liked the negative attention. Monique could recognize that now. He always wanted to argue and fuss about trivial things. And it had been getting worse.

"It was just a reason for him to runoff with the trollop he was tonguing down. Asshole," Monique ranted into the quiet interior of her car.

Monique decided right then and there that she would move on for good. No going back, no keeping Damon on standby. No more hoping. She wouldn't act like a cast member off of *Love and Hip Hop*. She would be a grownup. *A petty one, but a grownup all the same.*

Monique flashed her lights to get the couples' attention, and when they finally broke their passionate embrace to look in her direction, she honked her horn and waved. Damon's face was frozen in shock, but Monique couldn't see the woman's face because her hand was shielding her eyes. It didn't matter who she was anyway. Monique no longer cared.

Monique flipped them the bird before she backed out of the driveway. She sent Damon a breakup text and blocked his number. She was going to ghost his ass so hard her new name was going to be Casper.

"It's okay not to have everything right now, Moni. Prioritize, strategize, and win. It's over and done with. Focus on building your company. Don't cry over that piece of shit." Monique talked to herself the entire ride home, but the tears still flowed down her cheeks.

8

MAKING PLANS

I t had been over a week since Pearson had had any real contact with Monique. She barely came to his office, and if something needed to be handled, she sent her PA, Blake.

Pearson couldn't take the silent treatment much longer, especially since his private investigator had finally gotten back to him. Pearson had discovered quite a few interesting details about Monique's personal life, and he was pretty sure that she was in the dark about most of them. He wanted a chance to talk to her, but she seemed to be freezing him out. And Pearson wanted to know why.

Pearson was already borderline obsessed with Monique before the charity event, but after witnessing her magic in that silver dress, he was a complete goner. He hated the fact that she had chained herself to a man who was so unworthy of her love. Pearson noticed right off the bat how condescending Damon was. He also noticed the sly looks between Damon and Ashley.

When Pearson saw both Damon and Ashley leaving the dinner tables at the same time, he became suspicious. Pearson had cut his quality time alone with Monique short just to confirm his feelings.

Pearson had left the large ballroom and rounded the corner of the long hallway. He wished he could say what he saw was surprising, but it wasn't. Ashley and Damon were having what looked like a heated argument in the darkened hallway. The two were too far away for him to hear exactly what they were discussing, but from their body language, Pearson could see the passion.

Pearson waited like a stalker in the shadows for Ashley to leave, and once she was gone he confronted Damon.

"Just what the hell do you think you're doing? Slinking around with your girlfriend's sister?" Even though Damon was standing in his way of pursuing Monique, Pearson was mad that this man was going to break her heart. And the last thing Pearson wanted was for the object of his desires to be hurt by anyone.

"Who the hell are you to question me?" Damon clenched his jaw angrily.

"I'm someone who cares about Monique obviously, more than you do." Pearson took a menacing step forward.

"You don't know what you're talking about and you sure as hell don't know Monique. What you need to do is mind your business." Damon also took a step forward, not backing down from Pearson's threatening stance.

"I know if you don't tell Monique about you and her sister, I will," Pearson warned the other man.

"Fuck you! Like I said mind your business. Ain't shit goin' on between me and Ashley. And you better stay away from my girlfriend."

When Damon tried to brush past Pearson, he grabbed a hold of the front of Damon's tuxedo jacket and pushed him up against the wall, Damon tried to resist as the two men scuffled. Damon was finally able to push Pearson's hands away. Damon stalked away, but before Pearson could stop him, he saw people walking past.

Pearson rubbed the back of his neck. He had lost control again. There was no way in hell that as a grown ass man he should be fighting at a fucking charity event. He knew that there was press crawling all over the place, and all one had to do was snap the right picture, and there would've been nothing anyone could do to save his reputation.

Pearson took a deep breath to control in his temper. If he didn't do something about his feelings soon, he was going to fuck up his entire world. Unacceptable. I'm not eighteen anymore. Control yourself Grant.

Once Pearson had calmed down, he went back into the ballroom. He didn't know how he was going to sit across from the other man without ripping his head off, but he would do his best.

In the end, it didn't matter because Monique and her date left shortly after Pearson had returned. The tension was palpable and they haven't spoken since. Pearson had no idea if Damon did the right thing and told her what was going on or not, but he had the sneaking suspicion that the man would do anything in his power for Monique not to find out what happened.

Pearson had gone way past obsessed with his fixer, and he was glad that in the past week his company had kept him busy. He was finally caught up with all of his meetings, and the new application was in the final stages of production. He had even dropped a couple of spots on the trending topics lists even with snippets of his rant against the reporter going viral. But even with all of that going on in his professional life, Monique clouded his thoughts to the point of distraction.

So Pearson made a plan. He would do everything in his power to get the woman that he was enraptured by. Boyfriend be damned. Anything that stood in his way, he would crush. He was a fucking shark in business, and he was even deadlier in bed. Taking things nice and slow had never been his style so why mess with perfection.

Yes. Pearson had a plan, and he couldn't wait to put it in motion. He couldn't wait to get the beautiful goddess in his bed. He could picture her soft brown skin glowing against his stark white sheets. The paleness of his skin intertwined with the darkness of hers. He couldn't wait to have her underneath him, on top of him, hell he would take her any way he could.

BUT BEFORE HE could put his plan in motion for Monique, he would first have to end things with Stacy. Pearson hadn't seen her since he had booted her out of his place more than two weeks prior. He was glad that she stopped trying to act like his girlfriend. She knew the deal; they all knew the deal. Girlfriend wasn't in Pearson's vocabulary.

Thank God she finally got the message that she was temporary. Just like all the rest.

"Kelsey, I need you in my office." Pearson called his personal assistant. Within a few seconds, she was entered his office door.

"What can I do for you, sir?" Kelsey dutifully closed the door behind her. She took a seat with a tablet ready to take notes.

Pearson smirked. "You can drop the sir. Nobody is here in the office but us."

Kelsey smirked back. "Yeah okay. But I have to keep it professional at all times. I don't want to slip up."

Pearson laughed at the comment. "You're too good at what you do to slip."

"You're right." Kelsey smiled. "So what's up?"

"I need you to send Stacy Reid flowers and a tennis bracelet from Bvlgari."

"Hmmm. Okay. When would you like for the gifts to be sent?" Kelsey questioned, her professionalism back in full effect.

"Today if possible. If not, no later than tomorrow evening. I want this done ASAP. Pay extra if you have to."

"Will do. Do you want a message to accompany the gifts?"

"The usual message is fine, Kels. Thanks."

"Alright. I'm on it." Kelsey stood and headed toward the door. Pearson nodded as she left to do his bidding. It was great having someone you could trust no matter what.

Pearson rubbed his hands together diabolically. He was now closer to having Monique beneath him, he smiled wickedly at the thought.

THE NEXT DAY, Pearson's name stayed out of the news, and again Blake, Monique's PA, had shown up to discuss upcoming events. Pearson didn't mind dealing with Blake, she was a very thorough individual who Monique obviously had trained very well. He was just annoyed that Monique seemed to be avoiding him. It didn't matter, in the end Pearson would get what he wanted because he always did.

Pearson was going through the specs of the new application when Keifer came sauntering into his office. He and Keifer had known each other since college. Keifer came on board a few years after Pearson had started Media Tech Innovation. And even though Pearson threatened to fire Keifer several times a day, Keifer took it all in stride and never batted an eye over Pearson's volatile nature.

"Hey, Pearson, I wanted to let you know the promotion for the new launch is on schedule. My team is working to secure a high profile venue as soon as the release date is confirmed for the new communications app." Keifer sat down in the comfortable leather chair in front of Pearson's desk, and he knew this wasn't just about the new app.

"Okay. We will confirm the release date by next week. I also want to announce the new division at the launch party," Pearson said, placing the files he was looking over to the side.

Keifer nodded. "That's a good idea. So this will be announced at the department head meeting, I assume."

"Yes, I want to make sure the date is set first. I need Mark to be here first. He's still traveling." Pearson's vice president was overseas handling a deal with a Dutch company. The man was an invaluable asset and Pearson was happy to have him.

Even though Mark was a huge benefit to his company, Pearson was glad that his VP was still out of town. Although things seemed to be working out for Pearson, Mark would've definitely been too tightly wound to be of any benefit. It was a surprise the man had lasted for the five years he had been in the position.

"Okay, then I guess we are all set." Keifer nodded, but didn't move. Pearson knew that he wanted to talk so he sat waiting patiently.

Keifer sighed heavily. "So what did you do to Monique?" he finally questioned with furrowed brows. "She barely comes here anymore and she's been calling me direct."

It was Pearson's turn to wear furrowed brows. He'd had no idea that Monique was contacting Keifer.

"Why is she contacting you?" Pearson could barely contain the growl that wanted to come out. He hated that his want for this woman was so strong.

"She wanted to make sure I was aware of the schedule of events and that there weren't any marketing events for the company that she wasn't aware of. But the fact that she called and didn't come by is what has me confused," Keifer answered.

"Well, I'm confused too. She hasn't said much to me since the banquet over a week ago. She was fine before she left with her *boyfriend*." Pearson sneered. He couldn't keep the disdain out of his voice even if he tried.

Keifer frowned. "I never liked that guy."

Pearson perked up. He knew that Keifer and Monique used to work at a PR firm together before he started to work with Pearson, but he didn't know just how well they knew each other. If he wasn't so secretive about his plans, Pearson could've pumped Keifer for information. But he knew that his friend would try to discourage him from pursuing the object of his desire.

"So you know this Damon character?" Pearson questioned, trying hard not to sound too eager.

"Not really. I've met him in passing at different events. But he just always seemed a little shifty to me," Keifer responded with a shrug.

"Hmmm. Is that why you always seemed so eager to touch and caress on Monique every chance you get?" Pearson didn't mean to let his feelings about Keifer's unnecessary touching slip, but he couldn't help himself. Keifer was way too touchy feely with Monique.

Keifer's smile grew and he sat up in his chair. "I don't caress Monique."

"You do," Pearson disagreed.

Keifer's smug smile was starting to annoy him. "I don't. She's a sweetheart. I just want to make sure she feels supported and comfortable when she's here. You have to admit you can be a bit intimidating."

Pearson could see the logic in his friend's words, but he was too stubborn to agree that he was indeed intimidating, and when he wanted something as much as he wanted Monique, he could be downright aggressive.

"Well, maybe if you stopped touching her, then she would come around again." Pearson grunted, and Keifer had the nerve to laugh.

"All your little comments make so much more sense now. You like her!" Keifer accused.

Pearson shrugged, and Keifer's smile fell from his face as he shook his head.

"No. You need to leave her alone."

"No. I don't." Pearson smiled. No point in hiding his intentions now. Keifer would find out sooner or later that Monique would soon be his.

The rest of the conversation didn't go as smooth as Pearson would've liked, but Keifer would get over it. He would just have to accept that he had no say so whatsoever over Pearson's love life.

After another full day, Pearson walked into the restaurant to meet his longtime friend, Dominque Holmes. Dom was his private investigator, and all around information guru. He was also one of the secret weapons that nobody, not even Keifer, knew about.

As soon as Pearson sat down, Dom slid a folder full of pictures over to him. He looked at the photos with disgust. He wanted to throttle the man who was so blatantly cheating on Monique.

"They broke up the other night," Dom said, his deep voice smooth as the whiskey he'd sipped.

Pearson couldn't help the smile that crossed his face. "Did she find out about this?" Pearson asked, pointing at the pictures.

"She definitely caught him, but I doubt she knows about this."

"Fuck."

"Yeah. It's pretty shitty. Let me know if you need me." Dom nodded his head, the dark blue black locks fell in his crystal blue eyes as he tapped the bar and left.

Pearson was sipping on his drink and contemplating his next move when a husky voice he recognized gained his attention.

"Fancy seeing you here."

Pearson was surprised to see the woman. He had never met her before the other night, and it seemed too convenient for her to be in a place he frequented, but had never seen her before, especially after what he had witnessed, he wondered about the woman's intentions.

"I wouldn't actually call it fancy." *Suspicious maybe...* Pearson raised an eyebrow at the woman.

"Well, this is a fancy place, and you seem like a fancy guy." She smiled as she sat down beside him.

"Uh huh. So, what brings you here on this fine evening?" Pearson made small talk, but he really wanted to know why she was here.

"Just meeting a friend for drinks. And what brings you here?"

Pearson held up his drink and sipped in response.

She smiled and nodded. "You don't mind if I have a drink with you, do you?"

Pearson shrugged and waved over the bartender for her to order a drink.

The woman smiled widely and then caressed his bicep. Pearson knew when a woman was flirting, and he couldn't say that he was against female attention. However, flirting with this particular woman was not something he wanted to do.

"Are you flirting with me?" He smirked. The woman was bold, and Pearson couldn't believe her audacity

"You're a handsome man. Why wouldn't I?" She smiled seductively.

"And you're a beautiful woman," he couldn't help but acknowledge.

"So, why don't we get to know each other better?" She leaned closer to him, licking her lips.

Pearson sat back and stared at the boldness of the woman. He had only met her once and it was brief and awkward, so he didn't have any idea what she was playing at.

"I don't think that's a good idea. What would your sister think, Ashley?" he questioned.

Ashley waved her hand dismissively. "This has nothing to do with my sister. This is about me and you."

"Well, like I said I don't think it's a good idea." Pearson would've said that he didn't like mixing business with pleasure, but that wasn't strictly the case. He had plans to mix business with her sister's pleasure, and nothing was going to get in the way of that. Not even her sexy younger sister.

"Suit yourself. But the offer stands." She smiled as she sipped her drink seductively.

Ashley Carter is definitely trouble. I just wonder what she's really doing here.

9
_____

KEEP IT PROFESSIONAL

"Hey, Moni, isn't that Ashley? And isn't that *your* Pearson?" Venus asked as they followed the hostess to their table.

"I don't have a Pearson," Monique grumbled.

However, Monique's head swiveled around, searching until her eyes connected to a pair of emerald irises that she swore to herself she hadn't missed all week. After her breakup with Damon, she just wasn't feeling like herself. Monique had known deep down that he had been cheating on her, but because she felt an immense amount of guilt for her unsavory thoughts about Pearson, she kept sweeping her feelings to the side. *I'm such a fool.*

Logically she knew that her thoughts about Pearson didn't correlate to her break-up with Damon. However, she still couldn't help the feelings of guilt that clouded her mind. In order to feel exonerated from her shameful thoughts, she had very little contact with her biggest client for the past week. Monique just wanted to put some distance between her wayward thoughts, and the man that was the cause.

However, seeing Pearson sitting with Ashley like they had known each other for years rubbed her the wrong way.

"Venus, you go ahead. I'll be right there." Monique walked toward the two with fire burning in her eyes.

Monique didn't want to think that her sister had ill intentions, but with her little sister's track record, Monique had her suspicions. *I shouldn't be jealous, he's not my man. But what the hell is she doing here? Popping up again!*

"Hello. It's funny seeing you two here *together*." Monique greeted, sarcasm dripping from every word.

"Monique, it's nice to *finally* see you again," Pearson replied in a dry tone.

Ashley quirked a brow, but Monique noticed her usual smirk was suspiciously absent. Monique refused to address Pearson's sly remark. She knew why she was trying to keep her distance from the gorgeous tyrant, but she would be hard pressed to admit that to anyone else.

"I didn't realize you two had become so close in the past week." Monique looked back and forth between them with a slight frown on her pretty face.

Monique couldn't help but notice when Pearson's blank look morphed into a wicked smile. "I just ran into Ashley by pure coincidence. This is the first time I've seen *either* of you since the charity event."

"Oh." Monique looked away in embarrassment. She didn't know what had come over her. She had never reacted so unprofessional in her life. She chalked up her irrational reaction to the fact that she had some unresolved issues with her sister.

"Well, as lovely as it was seeing both of you, I need to get going. You ladies have a good evening," Pearson stated with a wink before rising from his seat, but he didn't leave.

Pearson looked so good, that Monique had to stop herself from staring. His light blue suit covered his muscular physique to perfection, and as hard as she tried to stop them, her eyes roamed over his tall frame from head to toe. *Gotdamn!*

The man was a walking wet dream, and it took all of the willpower she possessed not to lick her lips. Instead, she took a deep breath to calm herself down, which in hindsight, was a mistake, because the move enveloped her with the spicy sweetness of his scent that made the fire in her belly grow out of control.

Once Monique's wayward eyes made their way back to his face, the desire in Pearson's eyes could not be denied. Monique took a quick step back, putting much needed space between them. Although she was now single, she wasn't the type of woman to lust after a client.

"I *will* see you tomorrow." Pearson's tone brokered no argument.

Monique nodded dumbly, but words refused to leave her completely dry throat. Pearson strode confidently away without a backwards glance, leaving Monique confused and a little over-whelmed. She stared after him unashamed until her sister's voice brought her out of her trance.

"You're staring at him like you want to take a bite." Ashley's annoying smirk was back on her face, and Monique rolled her eyes.

"I think you're projecting what you want to do." Monique looked her sister squarely in the face.

Ashley shrugged. "He is quite delicious. I could have him if I really wanted him."

"I'm sure." Monique stared at her sister. The audacity of the woman was almost incomprehensible.

"So, what are you doing in this part of town?" Monique questioned when her sister stared after Pearson like he was a five-course meal.

"I'm just getting a drink." Ashley sipped her drink with a neutral look on her face.

Monique knew that her sister was up to no good, but for the life of her, she couldn't figure out why.

"Um hum." Monique continued to try her best to read her sister, but there was no use. Her sister was always up to something, so there was no telling what she had up her sleeve.

"Anyway, what are you doing here? Drinking alone?" Ashley smiled. Monique had to wonder why she had asked her that.

"No. I'm not alone," Monique said slowly. "Venus and I thought we'd get a bite to eat. Why?"

"What? No Damon?" Ashley questioned, sarcasm dripping from every word. Her sister moved her head all around as if she were searching for him.

"Nope. We..." Monique paused. "Never mind. I need to go. Have a good night, Ashley." Monique left her sister sitting alone at the bar. She almost told Ashley about the breakup, but something inside of Monique didn't want to give her sister the satisfaction.

Monique didn't look back at her sister as she made her way to the table where her best friend was sitting. But the conversation ran over in her mind. Ashley was hiding something. And it made Monique wonder if it had been Ashley she saw with Damon.

Monique didn't want to believe that her sister was the one cheating with her now ex-boyfriend, but unfortunately she wouldn't put it past Ashley. Monique sighed. She really hoped her sister wasn't that low down.

At least she had gotten rid of Damon. He was her past, and she would never go back. Monique may have been foolish to sweep her intuition under the rug. But she knew that if it was her sister that was cheating with Damon, she wouldn't be able to take the betrayal or the heartbreak of that. She would never forgive her sister for something that trifling.

Deep down in her soul, she prayed that her sister wouldn't be that vindictive, but in all honesty, she really couldn't be sure. And that reality, made Monique sad.

IT WAS FRIDAY, and Monique was glad that the week was coming to an end. But the butterflies were wreaking havoc on her stomach at the thought of seeing Pearson. There was a golf tournament to raise funds for ALS research the next day, and she needed to go over some details with him. And since he made it quite clear at the restaurant the night before that he wanted to see her, she knew that she wouldn't be able to avoid the meeting.

Monique admired her reflection in the elevator. She told herself that she'd only worn the olive wrap dress that fit her body to perfection, because she needed a boost in confidence. It had nothing to do with the fact that she was seeing Pearson and desperately wanted to impress him. *Nope, I don't want to impress a man. I don't need a man right now.*

Monique stepped off the elevator and made her way down the hall toward Kelsey, Pearson's PA. She repeated a pep talk in her head that she wouldn't act like a breathless bimbo when she got in his presence. She would be strong, capable, and strictly professional.

"Hi, Kelsey. I have a meeting with Mr. Grant. Is the conference room open?" Monique smiled, her professional mask firmly in place.

"Hello, Ms. Carter. Mr. Grant is waiting for you in his office. You can go on in." Kelsey smiled in return.

Monique frowned, her mask slightly slipping. They'd never met in his office before. She had been working with Pearson for over two weeks, they had one more week left before his interview was scheduled to run on tv, and although she avoided him the week before, she made sure that her assistant was there if anything came up. So having a meeting in his office felt like she was being sent to see the principal.

"Okay." Monique knocked on the closed door. She entered after the deep voice called for her to come in.

"Hi. Are you ready to go over your schedule?" Monique asked tentatively.

"Yes. Give me one second." Pearson continued to type on his computer without glancing in her direction. "Oh, could you shut the door please," he asked as he finished up what he was doing.

Monique closed the door, and the click seemed to reverberate around the large office. She had no idea why she felt the need to fidget like a teenager, but she had to give herself another pep talk just to walk on her trembling legs. Monique sat down quickly in a chair by a large conference table taking a deep breath to calm her nerves.

"I'm glad you could make it to the meeting today." Pearson's voice sounded seductive, and Monique knew her overactive libido had to be causing her to hallucinate.

She cleared her throat and gave him a small smile. "You requested my presence today, so..." She held out her arms. "Here I am."

"I didn't realize that's all it took. A request from me." Pearson's face was blank, but his voice still held that alluring tone.

"Yes, that's all it would've taken. Although *all* my clients are important, your situation is unique, so my availability is crucial. There were other things that needed my attention. I apologize if you felt neglected, that wasn't my intent." Monique responded in the utmost professional tone.

She noticed the slight frown on Pearson's handsome face before it went back to the emotionless mask he'd worn before. He then nodded his head as if he'd come to some conclusion and gave her a heart-stopping smile.

"Well, since all it takes is a request, then tomorrow I would like for you to accompany me to the golf tournament." Pearson kept smiling and at that moment, Monique couldn't think of a reason why she shouldn't go with him. *Oh yeah... client! I'm a professional. Keep it professional.*

"We need to work on finding you a date to these events. After that interview is aired, you will still have to do damage control. So did you have anyone else in mind?" Monique avoided answering his request.

She already had enough problems with keeping her distance, even with him being a not so nice guy. She couldn't stand to see him being friendly and accommodating at another charity event like he was with the kids at the STEM function. When she saw him with the little girls laughing and joking, her heart melted. If anything like that happened again, her resolve would fly out the window along with her panties.

"I just asked you to be my date. We don't need to think of anyone else," Pearson answered, his eyes darkening.

"Well, as I stated previously, I don't think it's a good idea for me to accompany you. You're my client," Monique responded logically.

"And you have a boyfriend?" Pearson stared at her, and Monique shifted uncomfortably in her seat.

"You don't need to worry about that," Monique stated dismissively. "The main thing is you're my client and how that might look if anyone were to find out."

"You see; I was thinking about that. Nobody knows I'm your client. We've been seen together way before the story broke, so I think that we should keep being seen together. That way, people can't assume that you're working for me." Pearson smiled devilishly, and Monique could see his weird sense of logic.

"I suppose it might not be a problem." Monique responded hesitantly.

Most of her clients didn't want it known that they needed her services, which is why she was able to charge such an enormous amount of money. It was a win-win in most cases, but it seemed that Pearson wanted to do things differently.

"But what if the media does question our connection? Are you willing to let it be known that the great Pearson Grant needed a fixer?" Monique questioned curiously.

Pearson shrugged his broad shoulders. "I don't think it would ruin anything."

"So what then? You want to just broadcast that I'm working to fix your reputation?" she asked with a frown.

"We don't have to answer them; you know? We can let them assume what they must," Pearson responded placing his hands on top of the table.

Monique shook her head. "I don't like that idea. They're thirsty and the more we evade them, the more someone will dig, and eventually they will figure it out."

"Fine. If they figure it out, then we won't deny it. But what's the harm in leading them to think something else?"

The idea could work, but deceiving the press was not something Monique wanted or looked forward to doing. If it backfired, the repercussions could be devastating to both their reputations.

"Lead them to believe something else like what? Like we're

dating?" Monique questioned. She would do just about anything for her clients, but she wasn't sure she was willing to go that far.

"I'm just saying that it will be safer not to bring anyone else in on this image debacle. I would feel more comfortable if you were the person with me at these stuffy events to keep me in line. If the press asks who you are, I can just ask for privacy or say no comment."

Monique softened at the idea just a tad at his explanation. She had to admit that his plan sounded solid, and she could keep an eye on him without people getting suspicious, and asking who she was.

I hope I don't regret this.

"Okay. I will be your date. But on one condition." Monique pointed her manicured finger at Pearson.

"What's that?" Pearson's smile grew across his handsome face.

"We keep this strictly professional. Both of our reputations could be ruined. Neither of us can afford to have this backfire."

"Keep it professional. Yeah, I can do that," Pearson responded quickly, but from the wicked grin that spread across his face, Monique was pretty sure she wouldn't be able to trust his words.

10

MAKING IT PERSONAL

Pearson was obsessed with getting Monique to let down her walls. Her insistence on being professional was like waving a piece of meat in front of a ravenous beast. He would make it his mission to have Monique. *She will be mine.*

Pearson didn't miss the subtle glances, and the hitch in her breathing at his seductive tone. He smiled wide knowing that he wasn't the only one affected by their banter or nearness to one another. Anytime she was in the same room with him, her sweet scent over took his senses and made him dizzy with lust.

He had never wanted a woman so bad in his entire existence. Pearson never really had to try that hard to get women. Even though his personality was not desirable or in the least bit charming, women seemed to flock to him. They all wanted to be the one to change him from the asshole to the sweetheart. *That shit will never happen.* Pearson scoffed at the thought.

He had lots of women try to "open him up," but what they all failed to realize, it wasn't a façade that Pearson put on. He wasn't trying to keep women at arm's length, or compensating for some fucked up childhood. None of that was the case. He liked being a loner. He found solace in programming and the least bit of social interaction as possible. People considered his behavior as him being an asshole, but people in general irritated him, and he acted accordingly. He didn't especially care how others may view his attitude. At least he didn't before Monique.

Pearson hated the way she hesitated to keep her words measured and professional around him. He had an idea it was so she wouldn't "set him off" or some other asinine idea that Keifer had probably put in her mind.

Speaking of which, Keifer stood laughing and smiling with Monique for the millionth time that day. They were at the charity golf event at a new indoor driving range. The place was immaculate with a large open seating lounge, a restaurant, and a bar. The high tech driving range wowed the crowd, and Pearson had to admit he was impressed. The indoor setting was perfect for the time of year even though the weather was fairly warm still in Dallas in November.

All of the driving competitions were over, so everyone was now schmoozing, and rubbing elbows. And although Pearson was supposed to be socializing, he couldn't help his eyes from finding Monique no matter where she was in the room.

It wasn't that she was extraordinarily dressed. In fact, Monique was dressed like every other woman there. She showed up wearing a little white skirt with a yellow, blue, and white argyle printed sleeveless shirt. Her shoulder length hair was swept up in a ponytail, and her face held a minimum amount of make-up. However, the outfit on her had Pearson subtly adjusting himself. Her thick thighs peaked tantalizing from her skirt, and the roundness of her ass couldn't be contained by the fabric that stretched across it. And it wasn't just her body. Pearson couldn't get enough of her unbelievably plump lips that were covered in a sheer gloss that made him want to slip his cock between them as he held her ponytail roughly.

Pearson shook his head he had to stop thinking about her sucking his cock before he embarrassed himself at this charity event.

"Well, if it isn't Pearson Grant." The voice was full of contempt, but it was just as irritating as it was the last time he'd heard it.

"I didn't think I would see you again after your little gift was delivered." Stacy sneered, her thin lips painted red to match her hair.

Stacy too was dressed in a little skirt and matching argyle shirt, except on her, the outfit was somehow lacking. Where Monique was all curvaceous and voluptuous, Stacy's body was lean with nothing to hold on to. Pearson had never thought he had a type before. A woman was a woman, but now all he looked for was plump, juicy lips and even plumper behinds. Something else Monique had changed.

"So I take it you didn't like the gift," Pearson responded, his tone calm. He hated confrontations, especially ones that were simply unnecessary.

Once he was finished with a woman, he sent a gift and flowers and that was it. Nobody in his past had shown any adverse feelings to his breakup methods. He would occasionally see an old companion, and they would be cordial, make small talk, and go on about their lives. He knew that Stacy would be a problem. *I should've let her go sooner.*

"The gift..." She scoffed. "No phone call or anything. Just flowers and a note. I'm worth more than that."

No. Actually, you're not.

Pearson so badly wanted to let the words slip past his lips, but he knew that Stacy would cause a needless scene, one she seemed to be dead set on causing anyway.

"Is there something that you need from me, Stacy?" Pearson questioned in a low voice. The people mingling and having mindless conversations didn't seem to notice the volatile situation happening right beside them. He wished his *date* would come and save him from the unnecessary foolishness. *Where the hell is Monique?*

"I need for you to have a fucking heart. How could you treat me so callously? Me?" Stacy's face seemed to be turning almost as red as her hair, and her voice began to rise. Pearson was way beyond annoyed at the little tantrum she was set on throwing. If Stacy caused Pearson to look bad in front of this particular charity, she would have hell to pay.

"Listen—"

"Pear? Hey, I need you to come meet some people." Monique's

voice cut off his tirade before it even started, and he didn't miss the little nickname she'd thrown out either.

He smiled when he saw her look Stacy up and down with a blank expression, but those fiery brown orbs told of the jealousy that he hoped she felt. *Interesting.*

"Okay, *Moni.*" Pearson smiled, throwing a nickname back at her.

"Pear? I thought you hated when people called you that?" Stacy snarled, giving Monique a hateful glare.

"I hated when *you* called me that, Stacy," Pearson replied without hesitation. But Stacy wasn't wrong. He hated when people shortened his name *usually.*

Stacy put her hands on her slender hips, and Pearson knew she was about to blow a gasket. He braced himself for the name calling and the shouting and the inevitable scene that would have him as a trending topic once again.

"Stacy, is it?" Monique gave her a smile that was predatory. Pearson should have been worried, but instead, he was mesmerized by the sight. "Stacy, I can understand your need to have Pearson's attention. However, the scene that you're trying to cause will not be good for you. Pearson just announced a large donation to the ALS foundation. He was just photographed with the children of a recipient. Now, you wouldn't want to be the woman yelling at such a charitable man, would you?"

Stacy pursed her lips, but she didn't respond. Pearson knew that Monique had hit her where it hurt. Stacy's father was Wilson Reid of Reid and Stone Attorneys at Law. Stacy Reid was a spoiled daddy's girl that got everything she wanted. She was also a party girl that was still in her everything was "fun" stage, even though she was in her late twenties. However, Pearson didn't mind because she was just another companion, and with her father's reputation, Pearson thought that she would know how to be discreet.

Pearson knew that her father had an image to maintain just like he did. If Stacy was at a charity function yelling and throwing a tantrum, her father would have her head on a platter.

Stacy narrowed her eyes. "You're not even worth all of this. Just wait. I'm sure your flowers and gift will be in the mail next week," Stacy spit hatefully at Monique before stomping off in a huff. Pearson was glad to see her go.

"Pear?" He smiled at Monique as she watched a sulking Stacy storm away.

Her perfectly arched brow rose on her beautiful face. "I can see that she was one of your *friends*." Monique coughed, and Pearson had the feeling she was covering a laugh. "I noticed you needed backup. That is what I'm here for, after all. I could tell you were on the verge of blowing."

"So you called me Pear?" Pearson wouldn't let go of the fact that the nickname sounded so natural coming from her.

"Yes. Now, although I wanted to get rid of Little Red Riding Hood, I still need you to meet a few people." Monique smirked, and he smiled.

Pearson didn't know what had transpired between them, but he felt closer to Monique somehow. And he liked the feeling.

"So, is she going to be a problem?" Monique asked as they walked toward an open patio slightly away from the hustle and bustle of the party.

Pearson thought seriously about the question. He really wasn't sure if Stacy was going to be an issue or not. She had already proved that she was unpredictable, Pearson would've never guessed that a party girl wouldn't just bow out gracefully.

"I'm not sure," he answered honestly.

"Okay. What's her last name?"

"Reid. Stacy Reid is her name. Her father is Wilson Reid," Pearson added with a grimace.

"Of the Reid and Stone firm?" Monique asked with narrowed eyes.

Pearson nodded.

"I will handle it." Monique sighed as she typed something into her phone.

Pearson noticed that she was always typing on her phone, but he never knew what she was doing. Making notes, sending a text, putting out a hit. Hell, maybe he didn't want to know.

"Okay." He stepped closer to her. It was as if there was a tether pulling him toward her. Pearson didn't want Monique to feel uncomfortable, plus she had already given him the keep-it-professional speech. But it was something about her.

"What are you doing?" Her words were breathless, as she stared up at him with big doe eyes with her pouty lips parted slightly. He wanted to kiss her.

Pearson ran the back of his hand down the side of her face and then he tucked a strand of hair that had escaped her ponytail behind her ear. If he wasn't mistaken, she shivered.

"I wanted—"

"There you two are." Keifer's voice interrupted what Pearson was about to say, and he couldn't help the growl that left his throat. He was pretty sure that Keifer was being a cock blocker on purpose.

"We'll finish this later," Pearson whispered in Monique's ear as he took a step back. He didn't know if the khaki pants that he wore hid the bulge that had continued to grow in her presence, but from the wide eyed expression displayed on her beautiful face, she'd definitely noticed.

Pearson frowned at Keifer as he relayed the message that they were needed for the presentation of the tournament awards. Pearson couldn't care less about a stupid trophy because he only wanted to raise money for the foundation. But he put his discontent to the side, and put a smile on his face.

Showtime.

THE ALS GOLFING event had gone on without any more mishaps, and for that, Pearson was thankful. ALS research was near and dear to his heart because his mother had suffered from the disease, and even though he made contributions often, this was the first time he lent his name as a draw for the foundation.

He felt like a hypocrite, he was using the event as a way to show that he was a nice guy, but the fact of the matter was, he wasn't. But Monique convinced him that his contribution as well as his name would help the foundation, even if he got a little publicity out of the whole ordeal.

Pearson knew that she was just doing her job, a job that he was paying her heavily to do, so he reluctantly agreed. However, when it was all said and done he felt accomplished. They had raised over a million dollars, and he was thankful that Monique had been there to witness it all.

They'd had so much fun at the event together that he had asked her to lunch. He made the date under the guise that he wanted to discuss the details of the event and go over the soon to be aired interview.

He knew after his display of lack of control and almost kissing her, that Monique may have felt a little worried, but she'd still agreed. It was her job to keep it professional, and it was his mission to do anything but.

As a condition of their date, he agreed to meet her at the restaurant. Pearson didn't want to push her too far, so he wasn't his usual demanding self. He would let her think she was in control, and then he would slip in under her defenses.

Pearson saw her as soon as she stepped into the restaurant. Monique had an ethereal glow about her. Her presence was always other worldly to him. It was like she was floating on a cloud as she moved with grace toward him.

She was dressed warmly in a pair of knee high boots, and black pants. Her long sweater and coat draped on her effortlessly. Monique was fully covered from head to toe, and Pearson was still mesmerized by her.

"Hey, sorry I'm late." She smiled that shy smile, and he felt his hardened heart soften just a little bit.

"You're not late. Have a seat." Monique shrugged out of her coat, and Pearson pulled out her chair. She sat down gracefully, and he gently pushed her under the table.

"Thank you." Monique smiled politely.

Pearson didn't like polite Monique or professional Monique. No. Pearson liked breathless, blushing Monique.

They tentatively discussed the event from the day before, and the upcoming interview that Monique didn't seem to worry too much about. She told him that with his ongoing media training that he would be ready for a counter interview on the same day on another station. Pearson wasn't too thrilled at that news, but he understood the strategy behind it.

"I think that the golf tournament was a success, and you being there with me helped a lot."

"Yes, I agree." Monique smiled again, and Pearson couldn't help but want to keep the expression on her beautiful face.

"There was another event that popped up for this weekend, and I was wondering if you would accompany me?" Pearson smiled, trying to put her more at ease.

"Oh? Keifer didn't mention any more promotional events." Her expression was confused and he knew why. Pearson didn't want any interruptions from anyone on this outing, especially not cock-blocking Keifer.

"I hope you're available," Pearson pressed.

"Yes, I can make sure I'm available. What type of event is it?"

Pearson hadn't thought that far in advance. He just wanted to get Monique alone. He thought quickly about the events that Kelsey had mentioned he had previously turned down. When the perfect event popped into his head.

"It's a technology banquet. Black tie. I usually skip it, but I think it's a good idea to attend this year."

"Great. Just have Kelsey give Blake the details and we'll make sure you're seen in a positive light."

Monique smiled and he knew that being agreeable to all of her positive image talk would keep her at ease.

They got back on the subject of the interview that would air the next week. She explained that the original conservative network would air his rant on their top slot. Monique scored a competing interview to be aired earlier, then repeated during the original rant. She also wanted him to talk about what he said, and she had a clip of his rant. It was genius really. She was taking all of their ammunition and using it against them. When they finally aired the interview, it would be old news.

Her intelligence and passion made Pearson want her even more. And he couldn't wait until the weekend to get her alone.

PEARSON THOUGHT that he would be able to handle having Monique all to himself. But he quickly discovered that it was an exercise in his willpower.

First, she stepped out of her house looking like a vixen in an off the shoulder, curve hugging, black floor length gown with an alluring slit up one side. Then she had the nerve to keep all of her focus on him. Now, Pearson knew that it was her job to be attentive to him as her client, but it felt like something more, and his lust just couldn't be controlled.

"Why do you skip this event every year? It seems like a really big deal." Monique leaned over and whispered in his ear as the speaker of the night addressed the crowd.

Pearson basked in her closeness, her sweet breath fanning across his neck made him want to take her lips right then and there. He shook his head to regain focus of the conversation.

"It is a big deal, but as you know, I'm not too big on social events."

Monique snickered. "Yeah, I guess you're right. But you know I've seen you act charming so I know that it's in you. You just have to try."

"I've been trying for *you*." Pearson touched her hand that was on top of the table, and tugged it toward him. He brought her hand to his lips and kissed it softly. "I'd do just about anything for you."

"Pearson, I-I..." Monique started, but he cut her off with a shake of his head.

"Not a conversation that we should be having at the moment." Pearson looked around and noticed a few stares shooting in their direction. "Tonight, we just go with the flow." He kissed her hand again and turned toward the speaker.

As the night went on, Pearson could tell that Monique had significantly relaxed. She smiled and laughed with the other guests and she made Pearson look like a social butterfly. If she weren't his date, there would be no way in hell he would've stayed and mingled.

Once again, Pearson had to admit, that he was having a good time at an event that he wouldn't have gone to. She even managed to pull him out on the dance floor, and that's when everything between them changed.

Monique's soft body pressed tightly against Pearson's and he relished in the exotic scent of her soft skin. His hands gripped her waist as he chastised himself for wanting to lower them onto her delectable derrière. He was damn near having an internal battle to keep his thoughts PG-13 and not X-rated.

"I've had a really good time with you tonight." Monique smiled up at him her glossy lips beckoning him to kiss them.

"I'm glad. You see how easy it can be once you stop fighting me?" He chuckled when she twisted her lips in a "whatever" expression.

"You mean if you stopped fighting *me*." Monique smirked up at him.

Pearson smiled. "How about we stop fighting each other?"

"Deal," Monique responded.

When she licked her lips temptingly, there wasn't a will on earth that could've stopped him from getting a kiss.

"I know I'm your client, but I can't help myself. I need to kiss you now."

Monique's doe eyes went wide and she audibly swallowed. But most importantly, she nodded.

"Thank God!" Pearson leaned down and took her lips in a passionate kiss.

He wanted their first kiss to be slow and seductive. He wanted to leave her breathless and wanting. But once he got a taste of her luscious lips, Pearson's hunger grew, and he ravished her mouth like a mad man.

Before the kiss could get too out of hand, Pearson slowed down from tasting every corner of her mouth to nibbling on her lips. *If the press is here, we're definitely a couple now.* He smiled at the thought.

"Go home with me." Pearson's voice was rough and ragged with desire.

"No." Monique was breathing hard.

"No?" Pearson smiled.

Let the chase begin.

11

BROKEN PLANS

"No?" Pearson smiled like she had told him yes.

"Yes. I mean no. You know what I mean, Pearson." Monique was flustered from the kiss as well as her heated body.

"I just want to be clear," Pearson stated his smile growing across his handsome face.

"It's clear that this was a mistake," Monique whispered, frantically looking around the room. Luckily, nobody was paying attention.

"That kiss was a lot of things, sweetheart, but a mistake is definitely not on that list."

"You're my client!" Monique shook her head.

She couldn't believe she let her guard down and had done something so unprofessional. She was a fixer and she was there to fix Pearson's reputation, not ruin her own.

"Monique—"

"No. Just please take me home. I'm really sorry." Monique turned and headed out the door with a determined Pearson hot on her heels.

"Moni, please wait." Pearson's soft tone made her pause. She'd never heard him sound so caring.

She slowly turned, feeling like a dramatic teenager. Monique couldn't believe that she tried to run out of a ball after being kiss like she was Cinderella. She wanted to roll her eyes at how much of a complete mess she was.

"I'm sorry that I made you so uncomfortable with my kiss that you ran." Pearson smiled softly, making her chuckle.

"I just don't think it's a good idea for us to get involved. You have so much more to focus on, and I was hired to help you." She shook her head with a frown. "Maybe this pretending to date was a bad idea after all."

"No. As a matter of fact, I don't think we should pretend. We should just see where this takes us." He stepped closer to her, grabbing her hand.

Monique stared at him in disbelief. Out of all the things he could've said, she wasn't expecting that. She tugged her hand, but he wouldn't let her go. She sighed heavily.

"You're just going to ignore everything I just said, huh?" She narrowed her eyes and shook her head. She always picked the stubborn ones.

"I could never ignore you." Pearson caressed the back of her hand slowly as he looked deep into her eyes. His orbs sparkled with mischief, and Monique couldn't resist the bright beautiful smile he gave her. Monique had to remind herself that this was a job. *Nothing else.*

"Why don't you escort me to the car, so that I can go home?" Monique stated cutting off all flirtation. She had to fight this attraction. She worked too hard for her career to flush it down the drain for a man. Albeit a sexy man, but a man nonetheless.

"Okay, Monique, I will take you home. But just know, the harder you run the faster, I will chase you." When Pearson leaned down and kissed the corner of her mouth, a shiver ran along her spine. *Damn him.*

THE LAST FOUR days had been uneventful for Monique. She had put in a call to Stacy's father, Mr. Reid, and after a little bug was put in his ear, he promised to rein in his wayward daughter. He sent Stacy on a trip to an island, so Monique knew she didn't have to worry about the redhead popping up and making trouble anymore. Now all she was worried about was her own troublemaking ways.

After her whirlwind date with Pearson, Monique just knew that their kiss would lead to nothing but trouble, especially after his threat to chase her down, she thought that she would have to avoid him. However, every time she was in the same room with him, Pearson was nothing but professional. The whole thing had Monique shook.

But she didn't have time to contemplate Pearson's hot and cold behavior, it could all mean nothing anyway. Because today was the day of the big interview, and if it all went to hell, she wouldn't have to worry about their working relationship because she would be out of a job.

"I must be cursed," Monique mumbled to herself as she paced back and forth. Pearson was supposed to be at the station a half an hour prior, and his cell was going straight to voicemail.

Monique tapped furiously on her phone. She was using every contact she had to stall the interview and try to get a hold of Pearson. If he didn't show, it could potentially ruin them both.

"Shit," Monique hissed under her breath when one of her contacts at the station texted her that the interview couldn't be postponed.

Monique knew that everything had been going well, and she let herself get comfortable. Keifer had warned her that Pearson was an unbearable beast to deal with, so she was weary of their interactions. However, little by little, Pearson had worn her down. He was on his best behavior when dealing with her. He showed up when she told him to, he acted accordingly, and didn't make a fuss. Even after their steamy date, he did exactly what she asked him to do. It was all a conundrum.

Monique was drawn to Pearson, no matter how big of a tyrant people said he was, or the cold callous way he dealt with others, she found herself gravitating toward him. She sighed at herself. She couldn't believe that she was in this situation.

She couldn't get the way that he'd kissed her out of her head. She tried to convince herself that the passionate touch of his lips and the zing of pure lust that hit her meant nothing. That his deep voice with the promise of more was nothing, and that the way her heart galloped in her chest was also... nothing. She was so disappointed but she knew she had to focus. There was too much at stake and she had shit to do.

Monique took a deep breath and gathered her thoughts. She dialed Keifer's number as she tapped her high heeled shoe on the linoleum tile of the TV stations decrepit greenroom floor. She would get in touch with Pearson by any means necessary.

However, when the voicemail clicked over, she could feel herself getting worked up, and she started to panic. Monique's self-doubt was getting out of control. It had been a long time since she had this much insecurity, but at every turn this case was getting harder to fix.

After her breakup with Damon, Monique had thrown herself into her work. She didn't want to think about another failed relationship, or the nagging feeling that her sister potentially had something to do with it. As usual, Monique didn't fix her own life, she just simply swept it under the rug to deal with later. Now here she was, unable to fix her client. She had never been in this predicament before, and she was close to losing her damn mind.

When she called Kelsey, Pearson's assistant and it went to voicemail, Monique decided to call Mark, the VP. He was always in and out of town, and Monique thought he seemed uninterested in the whole debacle, but maybe Mark could tell her where in the hell Pearson was.

"Hello?" Mark answered.

"Hi, Mark. This is Monique Carter. I was wondering if you have seen or heard from Pearson today?" she questioned, biting her nails.

"Uh, hi, Monique. I saw him earlier. He left the office about two hours ago. I haven't seen him since. Sorry."

"Two hours?" Monique's eyes went wide.

"Is everything okay?" Mark asked, sounding concerned.

"Everything is fine. Thanks, Mark." Monique disconnected the call quickly before he could ask any more questions. Mark seemed to be the nervous type, and Monique definitely couldn't deal with anyone else's nerves right now.

Monique sighed, and plopped down on the worn sofa in frustration. She looked at the clock, and sighed. The interview was scheduled in less than an hour, and Monique was at a loss for what the next step would be if Pearson flaked. If he didn't show up, her whole plan would go up in smoke.

Just when she was about to sink into the dark abyss of doubt, Monique's cell rang. The shrill tone snapped her out of her self-loathing, and back to reality.

"Monique Carter," she answered the private number, hoping against hope that it was Pearson or Keifer finally getting back to her.

"Ms. Carter, this is Kelsey Davis. I'm calling to inform you that Mr. Grant has been in a minor accident. He's currently being admitted to Baylor Medical."

Monique's heart stopped. "A-a- accident? If it was minor, why is he being admitted?"

"Well, Mr. Grant needed to be admitted for observation. He wanted to let you know so you could take the necessary steps to handle any problems that may occur."

After Kelsey relayed the details of what had happened to Pearson, Monique was relieved to find out that he wasn't seriously injured. But now, she had a bigger problem. The scheduled interview was still on the line and Pearson was definitely not going to make it.

"Thank you, Kelsey. I'll take care of everything," Monique responded.

"You are so welcome. Contact me if you need anything else." Kelsey disconnected.

Monique didn't have time to contemplate her despair. She had to get in gear and figure out how she would fix this new mess Pearson was in. She just knew that there wasn't any way she could make it to

Baylor Medical and back to the station before the interview was set to air.

"I swear I need teleporting abilities." Monique mumbled as she continued to pace.

Monique needed to move around to get her thoughts together. There was no way that she could cancel the interview. The other station would be airing Pearson's rant come hell or high-water, and they desperately needed to combat the effects of the interview with one of their own. Monique knew that they needed the interview. She just needed to tap into her black girl magic to figure out a solution.

Monique froze mid step. A smile that would have creeped out the biggest *Black Mirror* fan spread across her face. She knew exactly what to do, and it was going to work. *It's definitely going to work!*

It was a wonder why the idea didn't come immediately after Kelsey told her the details of the accident. "I'm losing my touch." Monique shook her head as her fingers instantly began to rapidly move over her phone. She had a lot of work to do and very little time to do it.

After contacting her assistant, the station manager, and Kelsey again, her plan was set in motion. Monique strutted out of the station with new pep in her step. Her new idea was even better than her initial plan, and Pearson was going to come out of this thing looking like roses after a spring rain.

"MR. GRANT, I want to thank you for sitting down with us after such a harrowing experience."

"Of course." Pearson nodded as he sat up with a wince.

"So it is our understanding that you were a victim of a hit and run." The male reporter was sitting at the edge of his seat, thoroughly enjoying the amazing scoop that he was receiving.

"Yes, that's correct." Monique rolled her eyes at Pearson's unwillingness to elaborate.

"Can you tell us a little about the incident?" the reporter probed.

"Well..." Pearson rubbed the back of his head in what Monique knew was a nervous tick of his. "I stopped to help a woman and her kids that were having car trouble when a driver that wasn't paying attention, side swiped their car. The lady was already in the middle of changing her tire, and when the other car hit hers," Pearson shook his head and sighed, "the tire flew off and grazed my ribs as I pushed the young woman out of the way."

"Wow, it's a miracle that no one was killed."

"Indeed." Pearson gave a semblance of a smile.

"Is everyone okay? I mean I see that you have quite a few bandages."

"I'll be fine. The young lady as well as her children weren't hurt."

"Well, you've had quite a day Mr. Grant, and we, here at TV Eleven, are glad you're okay."

Pearson nodded, and Monique knew that this was TV gold.

"Now, let's get down to the heart of why we really came to do this interview today."

"Yes. Let's." Pearson's face turned serious, and Monique had to give him the signal to relax. She didn't want him coming off as an uptight stick in the mud. They were trying to show a different side of him.

The accident was a blessing in disguise. Pearson came off looking like a hero who had stopped to help a single mother and her kids stranded on the side of the road while keeping them from enduring bodily harm when a reckless driver hit their car. It was a lucky coincidence that all of this happened on the same day as the interviews.

The rest of the interview went off without a hitch, and just like Monique had suspected, Pearson came across as down to earth and even likable. Now they could replay the story of the generous local hero instead of the millionaire jackass ranting about women.

Once the reporter and his crew left the hospital, Monique and Pearson were left alone. She finally felt at ease, the tension of the day slowly leaving her neck and shoulders.

Monique stretched lazily when she saw Pearson watching her

intensely. His eyes glowed with an emotion that she didn't want to decipher. It sent shivers up and down her spine.

"Uh. You okay? Do you need me to get a nurse or something?" Monique arched an eyebrow in Pearson's direction. There wasn't any way in the world that she was going to address that lustful look in his eyes.

"Yes. I'm fine. Are *you* okay? It looks like you need a massage." The way the word massage rolled off his lips made it sound dirty.

I like that shit. Monique shook her head and tried not to smirk. Only Pearson Grant could bring out the slutty thoughts in her.

"I just might need a massage after the worry you put me through today." Monique smiled, trying to lighten the mood.

"Yeah. Sorry about that. I guess you rubbed off on me." Pearson's eyes lit up again but this time they held a hint of embarrassment. He rubbed the back of his neck again nervously and Monique had to smile at how adorably boyish he looked in that moment.

"How did *I* rub off on you?" Monique asked curiously.

"You are the do-gooder type. And even though I kicked up a fuss, I had a great time at the charity event with you."

Monique smiled and her face heated when the memory of their lustful kiss flashed across her mind. She wouldn't dare admit it out loud, but she had a wonderful time with him as well. It had been a long time since she was able to go to an event and not have to worry about how her date would react or in Damon's case, overreact to something.

"So because I'm a *do-gooder,* you decided to help someone?" Monique was happy that she seemed to be making a good impression on him, and hopefully he was actually softening and not just trying to get into her panties.

"You know I've been thinking about our kiss."

Shiiiit. I've been thinking about it too, Monique thought, but on the outside her face remained passive as she responded, "Is that so?"

"Yes..." Pearson's words cut off as he winced again when he tried to sit up. "Could you adjust my pillow please?" He smiled.

Monique decided not to comment, and fluffed his pillow like a candy striper. When she leaned over him, Pearson took advantage, and kissed her softly on the neck.

For a few seconds, Monique reveled in the feeling before she came to her senses and jerked away. *Damn that felt good.*

"I thought we talked about this..." Monique said breathless. She could still feel the heat from his lips on her neck.

"No. You said we shouldn't, and I said we should." He smiled, flashing beautiful white teeth.

"That's because we shouldn't." Monique stood up straight, took a deep breath, and crossed her arms over her chest.

Pearson gently tugged her forward. "I could've been killed today. Don't I deserve a little sugar for my efforts?"

Monique giggled girlishly. "I thought you said it wasn't serious?"

"Look at me. All bandaged and bruised. I, at least earned a kiss. Come on, at the very least."

Monique looked around before she started to lean in, but right before their lips touched, Keifer slammed into the room.

"Pearson! Man, damn you scared the hell out of me! Mark said you were in the hospital because you got hit by a car." Monique couldn't help but feel annoyed, but she jerked back in time for him not to notice the hanky-panky that was going on between them.

It seemed like every time her and Pearson were alone, Keifer would interrupt them. Maybe it was a sign. Maybe it was for the best that they didn't pursue whatever this was between them.

"I'm fine," Pearson grumbled from the bed. "I just finished the interview, and now, we're waiting on the nurse."

"So how did the interview go? Will you still be crucified for your comments?" Keifer looked back and forth between the two of them with a smile plastered on his face.

Monique wasn't sure, but it seemed like Keifer enjoyed the fact that Pearson had gotten himself into a messy predicament. When Keifer came to her for help, he was essentially warning Monique that she wouldn't be successful. He was always making comments about how Pearson would be unwilling to do something, or how she should just keep him at arms-length because of his volatile moods. Now that she had worked with Pearson for a while, she noticed that he wasn't all that bad, she would have to pay more attention to Keifer's "warnings" and dissect what they really could mean.

"I'll let you guys catch up. Pearson, great job today. I'll check the ratings and the trending topics and keep you guys in the loop about how the interview went over with the audience. Get some rest, and I'll stay in contact." She gave them both her professional smile, and headed out of the room.

"Okay. And Moni?" Monique stopped and turned around to face both men. She would never get used to the sexy way Pearson said her name.

"Yes?" She questioned trying to hold onto her smile.

"Thanks for everything. Really." Pearson gave her a genuine smile, and for fucks sake her panties were instantly wet. *Well damn!*

"It's what I do." Monique winked and continued out the door.

12

UNDER SUSPICION

Pearson watched the graceful sway of Monique's hips as she left the hospital room. She was mesmerizing, but the man in front of him was not. *Cock blocker.*

Pearson would've been more upset at Keifer, but he had some things that he needed to share with the other man, and it couldn't wait.

"Man, you scared the shit out of me. I was in a meeting, and when I came out, I saw a ton of missed calls from Monique. I thought Mark was going to pass out when he relayed Kelsey's message."

Pearson chuckled, "Mark needs to fucking relax."

"Yeah, but you know how he is. But really, dude. I thought your ass was dead." Keifer stated with furrowed brows.

"No, but it wasn't for some asshole's lack of trying." Pearson responded with a frown.

"Yeah. People need to pay more attention. Stupid people texting and driving." Keifer shook his head his blond hair swinging with the gesture. "Did they catch the person?"

"No. And it's a shock with all the shit going viral these days that nobody saw a thing."

"Hmmph. Well, hopefully the police will catch his ass." Keifer frowned.

"Do you honestly think I would leave this up to the police?" Pearson questioned, his face brightening with vengeance. There was no way in hell he trusted the police to catch this guy.

"Uh. Yeah. It's their job, Pearson. You have to keep your nose clean and out of trouble. That means no running off to play vigilante justice on some unsuspecting sap that was probably just not paying attention, or simply driving without insurance." Keifer shook his head again his frown deepening.

"You watch too much late night television. Nobody is talking about being a vigilante. I just want to know who sent me to the hospital. That's all." Pearson saw the suspicion in his friend's eyes, but Keifer merely nodded without comment.

Pearson wasn't about to divulge any more of his plan to Keifer. He would just try to talk him out of doing what needed to be done. Keifer was on the cautious side, always weighing all the options before making a decision. Pearson on the other hand was a "just get it done" type of guy. Pearson knew that that car swerving into them on the side of the road was no accident. He may not have been the most observant person in the world, but Pearson knew the sound of a car accelerating. Whoever was behind the wheel of that car sped up as they got closer to Pearson standing on that roadside.

Pearson had felt like somebody had been lurking in the shadows around him for weeks. However, he just put that weird feeling to the back of his mind and focused on getting his image together and keeping his business from crumpling.

But now, after today's events, he could no longer ignore his gut. Somebody was trying to take him out, and Pearson was going to figure out who it was. *If it's me or them, you can bet for damn sure it ain't gonna be me.* Pearson thought as he lifted his bruised body from the hospital bed. First, he was going to get himself discharged, and as soon as he got himself together he was going to give a call to Dom, his private investigator and friend. Then, he was going to get some rest. It had been a long ass day, and Pearson was exhausted.

∼

"You think somebody tried to kill you?" Dom's deep velvety voice held nothing but seriousness.

Pearson wasn't the paranoid type, and never in his life had he ever thought that somebody would be out to kill him. Even with his not-so-nice dealings with people in both his professional and personal life, he never had the inkling that someone would want to hurt him. He'd been threatened a time or two, but nothing serious. It was just something that happened when you were a shark in business, and a ruthless lover. Pearson took it all in stride, but now, he had to take a closer look at those people that thought he did them wrong.

There had been so many women in his past, but not all of them thought he was a cold calculating bastard, even though, that's exactly who he was; at least to them. There had only been a few that made a fuss when their time had come to an end, but they usually faded into oblivion within a few weeks of him cutting them loose.

Now, his professional life would be much easier to narrow down his enemies. There were several board members that wanted him to step down as CEO of his own company. *Yeah, like that shit will ever happen.*

Then there was the business that he walked away from when he started his own. The owner Jeffery Mann hadn't been too impressed that his best programmer wanted to walk away and had essentially become his competition. Things especially got bad between the two men when Pearson's IPO went public and became almost a billion-dollar success over night.

Jeffery felt like Pearson had stolen technology and what should've been his success, Pearson had kept for himself. Jeffery tried to sue, but the case lacked enough evidence and was thrown out as frivolous. Jeffery Mann was not happy. He made it his life mission to try and undercut Pearson's company at every opportunity.

"I don't think Jeffery Mann would do this." Dom's dark gaze slid around the room with ease. To anyone observing the men, Dom would've looked calm and relaxed, Pearson knew better. Dominque Holmes was as lethal as they came.

"His potential to be a suspect is as good as anyone else." Pearson shook his head as he rubbed his hands through his thick locks.

"Nope. Not his style. He wants you destroyed publicly with your reputation and business ruined. Trying to kill you on the side of the road doesn't exactly get him what he wants."

"Hmmph." Pearson didn't want to admit that the other man made sense, but Dom was right. Jeffery Mann wanted him humiliated and broke, but dead... probably not.

"Your list of suspects will be too much for me to handle if you put all of your... companions on it." Dom smirked his cerulean gaze twinkling.

Pearson chuckled. "There are a few that need to be looked at, but I don't think any of the women I have dealt with would want me dead. At least I would hope they wouldn't."

"Listen, this is some serious shit. If you think somebody tried to kill you, I believe you. But your ass needs to lay low, maybe take an unscheduled trip where nobody knows where you're going."

"I could do that. There's a convention coming up that I never go to, might as well get some work done while I'm hiding." Pearson frowned.

"Not hiding. Staying safe, so that I can do what I do. Big difference." Dom stated, his tone steely with seriousness.

"Yeah, yeah whatever. I'll let you do your thing; you won't get any more hassle out of me." Pearson put his hands up in a surrendering motion.

"Did you tell the fixer about any of this?" Dom asked, his expression remaining serious. Pearson's frown grew deeper.

"No, I don't want her to get involved. She's got enough to deal with, with my reputation, there's no need to put more on her plate." Pearson shook his head.

"Did you tell her about the pictures?" Dom asked.

He was finally making head room with Monique. She was starting to trust him, and Pearson didn't want to throw another wrench into things. No, hell no! Pearson wasn't about to tell Monique shit.

"No, she broke up with him. There's no need to bring up old shit," Pearson replied still frowning.

"I hope that choice doesn't come back to bite you." Dom shook his head in disappointment.

Pearson waved off his concern. "None of her concern. I got this."

"Alright." It was Dom's turn to hold his hands up. "Like I said, it's your choice.

Damn right it's my choice. And I sure as shit will not jeopardize my future with Monique because some asshole wants me dead, or her asshole of an ex. Nope.

PEARSON'S RIBS were still sore from his brush with the flying tire, but his anger at the situation was keeping the feel of the bruises at bay. He had forwarded Dom all of the names of the suspects that could've been involved in some idiotic plan to hurt him.

What am I, in a fuckin' gangster movie? Pearson shook his head at the nonsensical idea. Nobody should've wanted him dead. His attitude wasn't one to be desired, but he had never in his life physically hurt another human being.

Pearson didn't have some dark and seedy past that was coming back to haunt him in some way. He was just a hard working guy that lucked up and got richer than he ever would've imagined. He was a law abiding citizen; no DUI's, no nights in jail, not even an unpaid speeding ticket graced his record. And although he dated his fair share of women, all of them were consensual and none of them were left unsatisfied. *So what in the entire hell?*

Maybe Keifer was right, maybe he was just being paranoid. However, he would definitely take Dom's advice and go out of town for a week or two. There were plenty of places that he could visit for business, and the upcoming conference in Vegas was the first place he would go.

Pearson started to formulate a plan that would kill a couple of birds with one stone if he played his cards right. He had been trying to get Monique out on a date without any real luck. Pearson wanted to be seen with her so once they began a relationship, it wouldn't be some sordid secret that he would have to keep for their respective reputations.

Monique Carter would never be anyone's secret, and she sure as fuck wasn't going to be his. Pearson wanted everyone to know that the magnificent beauty was his woman. He wanted men to be envious of the miraculous gift of a woman on his arm.

Pearson wanted to be worthy of a woman like her. He wanted to be worthy of *her*. Pearson picked up his cell and sent off a few text messages before he dialed Kelsey. She was his right hand and he didn't know what he would do without her.

The funny thing about Kelsey that almost nobody knew was that she was his younger cousin. He didn't trust just anybody with the knowledge and access that Kelsey possessed working for him. They kept it strictly professional in front of others, Pearson didn't want to give away the secret of her being family.

Kelsey picked up after just one ring. "Hello?"

"Kels, hey, I need you to do something for me," Pearson said eagerly.

"That's what you pay me for." Kelsey's tone was dry, but Pearson knew that she was smiling. His cousin had a wicked sense of humor that she hardly ever got to show.

"Yes, and I pay you plenty." Pearson answered his tone even drier than hers.

"Alright. So how may I serve you milord?" Kelsey said in a cheeky British accent.

Pearson chuckled. He was glad that she could lighten his dower mood. Even with his plan that would finally get him and Monique on the same page, Pearson still felt a little beaten down by the craziness that had been circling him lately.

"I decided to go to the Global Stage Tech Summit in Vegas. I need you to book a penthouse suite for the week. I also need you to book two first class tickets."

"No jet this time?" Kelsey asked, her professionalism switched back on without any hesitation.

"No. I don't think that will be a good thing at the moment. Commercial will be fine, besides it's less than a three-hour flight." Pearson hoped his voice conveyed the nonchalant attitude that he didn't feel.

Pearson didn't want to let Kelsey know that he felt like a saboteur was somewhere lurking. It was better to purchase last minute tickets, that way if somebody was trying to track him it would be harder. There was too much planning and logistics that went into flying private. He didn't want to take the chance of anyone finding out where he was going.

"Okay, I will arrange everything now. I will send you the itinerary and conference confirmation shortly." Kelsey cleared her throat nervously before continuing. "I'm guessing that Keifer isn't the second person accompanying you on the trip."

Pearson smiled. "You guessed right. The companion ticket will be for Ms. Carter."

"Okay. I'll text you the details." Pearson was almost certain that he could hear the smile in Kelsey's voice as she disconnected.

A week-long getaway ought to have Monique right where I want her, Pearson thought as a Cheshire like grin graced his handsome face.

He couldn't wait to convince the beautiful, sassy woman that he was the man for her.

13

NO REST FOR THE WEARY

onique was mentally exhausted when she finally made it to her home. The day's events had caught up to her as soon as she left Pearson's hospital room. The stress and worrying over Pearson was causing grey hairs to pop up. Monique sighed. She prayed for this; for a high profile client that would bring her the notoriety that she wanted. *I won't complain about answered prayers.*

Monique wished that she could just go in her house and relax with a glass of wine and a bath, but alas it was not to be. She promised Venus that they would go out for dinner and drinks no matter what. They hadn't seen each other in weeks, and Venus even agreed to go with Nikki coming, and that in itself was a small miracle.

The two ladies did not get along. No matter how neutral Monique tried to be, Venus and Nikki were just like oil and water. Often times, Monique would have to meet them separately just to hang out, but it looked like they would finally be able to put their differences aside for one night to give her some support.

When Monique pulled up to her house, it was safe to say she was more than a little shocked to see her sister. They hadn't spoken in forever, and the last time they had seen each other at their mother's, it was in passing. Monique made sure to be late, so that she wouldn't have to endure her mother babying her sister, and her sister being a grown ass brat.

"What are you doing here?" Monique couldn't keep the suspicion out of her voice if she wanted to. She and her sister had never really been that close. And the fact that Ashley had been popping up everywhere lately, had Monique feeling more than a little weary.

"Nice to see you too, *sis.*" Ashley all but sneered, and Monique shook her head. She almost felt guilty for not trusting her sister, that is until Ashley spoke and reminded Monique of all the reasons she didn't.

Sometimes family can treat you the worst. Keep your guard up Moni.

"Let's try this again. What do you want? Make it short and quick because I don't have the time or the inclination to deal with any bullshit right now." Monique tossed her purse straps over her shoulder and placed her fists on her ample hips.

She called it her Wonder Woman pose. It always signaled that she meant business and was not to be played with.

"Mama sent me over here to see what the hell has been wrong with you. I told her you were fine. Because you were the same ole' Monique. Walking around like your shit don't stink, lookin' down at everybody else." Ashley's lip curled up in disgust, and Monique wanted nothing more than to slap her in the mouth.

Sweet Lord, give me peace. Don't give me strength because I might kill her if you do. Monique prayed silently to herself before addressing her sister once more.

"Girl, if you don't get the hell off my porch with your mess. I'm tired, I have plans, and I know *my* mama knows better than to send you anywhere." Monique pushed past her sister to place her key in the door.

Monique didn't know what was wrong with the other woman, but she had already decided that loving her sister from a distance was the best way to go. Monique refused to jeopardize her sanity and peace because somebody happened to be related to her.

If her sister wanted to act as if they weren't blood, and treat her like shit on the regular, Monique was more than happy to oblige.

"Bitch..." Ashley started, but Monique had dropped her purse and was crowding Ashley before the other woman could blink.

"Let me tell you something. I'm not going to be not one more bitch or I'm going to slap the taste out of your mouth. Mama ain't here to protect you this time, and you're on my property. I will whoop the black off your ass without a second thought. Now, you're my sister, so you get a warning, but it's the last thing you will ever get from me. Get. The. Fuck. Off. My. Porch." Monique's anger was exposed with each snarled word. Her sister's hatred for her had shown through with every vile word she spewed in Monique's direction.

There was no love lost between the two of them, and Monique refused to be held captive any longer by the sense of sisterly duty for a woman that had no love for her whatsoever.

"See, that's why Damon is always paying somebody else attention. You think you're so much better than everybody with your mean ass. Well, your man loves to compliment me, always in my DM's and asking what I'm doing. Just ask him." Ashley's smile was positively cruel.

Monique wanted to lash out and scream at her sister that she was a liar, but something told her that Ashley was telling the truth. Her sister was vindictive that way. She would hold on to any bit of information that she could use against you until just the right time. She wanted that wound to be open and hurting when she struck.

"It doesn't matter who he compliments or DM's, we're not together. We haven't been for over a month. As a matter of fact, I'm surprised all he did was slide into your DM's with your sneaky ass. Did you take it further?" Monique threw the words at her sister with a fire blazing inside. She didn't want to believe that it was her sister on Damon's porch kissing him, but the way Ashley was acting.

Monique kept her expression blank because she refused to give her sister the reaction that she wanted. Yes, later Monique would rant and rave, and curse Damon's name, but not in front of her sister. Monique would never let anyone see her fall.

"So you think I'm that lowdown that I would fuck your man?" Ashley asked incredulously as if she hadn't just been bragging about his compliments. And the fact that she spent an entire dinner flirting and throwing herself at the man at her mother's house two months prior.

"Yes, yes, I absolutely think that. You do everything in your power to hurt me. I wouldn't put anything past you, Ashley. *Anything.*" Monique said without hesitation or guilt. It was time to get all of her feelings out on the table. *No time like the present.*

Ashley shrugged. "I can't help it that your man wants me." Ashley stuck out her arms then ran her hands down her body. "Just look at all this. Why wouldn't he want me?"

"What you mean is why *would* he want you, why would anybody want you? You're negative, ignorant, and jealous. You don't have anything good or nice to say about anything or anybody. And to be honest, I don't give a damn anymore. If you want to hate me, then so be it, but know this, if you did betray me, I will beat the shit out of you." Monique pointed an accusing finger at her younger sibling.

No matter what Monique said, Ashley would never see her own fault, she would never admit to the part she played in the demise of their sisterly bond. Monique was a big enough woman to admit that she should've and could've done better, but she didn't. That was something that Monique would have to deal with.

Ashley narrowed her eyes and pursed her lips angrily. It didn't matter how much shit her sister talked, she knew that Monique could back up everything she said. Even though Monique had grown, and was too classy to fight her sister on the front porch of her house, there was only so much one person could take.

Ashley wasn't crazy enough to test Monique's patience any further. She huffed and stormed off the porch toward her car. As she marched away she threw over her shoulder, "I didn't want Damon's funky ass anyway."

I swear this girl is not related to me.

Monique turned and went back into her house promising herself that she didn't care if Ashley and Damon went behind her back. But deep down she did care, and the reality was, if they did that would be the very end of her sister.

MONIQUE ALMOST CANCELED HER GIRLS' night out after the visit from Ashley. Monique hated to feel the nagging in her gut to find out the truth, and not just take her sister's words as bullshit. But something told her that Ashley and Damon had slept together.

Damn I need to fix my life.

Speaking of fixed, Monique had been getting updates all evening about Pearson. The interview seemed to have worked, and he was once again a trending topic, except this time, it was all positive. She was happy that she wouldn't have to worry about Pearson tonight. She shot him a text giving an update, and put her phone down to charge.

Monique started to get ready, and she tried to clear her thoughts as she did, but the more she thought about Ashley, the madder she got. Ashley always had something to say about her relationship with Damon, and she was always making little snide comments.

"I hope she didn't sleep with him. Surely she wouldn't do her own sister dirty not over some man," Monique stated out loud as she shook her head. She gave herself the once over in her mirror to make sure her make-up, hair, and outfit was on point. If she had to go out after the day she had, at least she could look her best.

Monique grabbed her purse and coat as she made her way out the front door. She grabbed her keys, and set the alarm on her way out. She didn't know if she would tell Venus about what Ashley said. But she really didn't want to hear her best friend say, "I told you so."

Venus warned her about letting Ashley slide with her comments and inappropriate behavior.

"But damn, she told my stubborn ass," Monique commented still talking to herself.

She was one of those people that had to hear herself say something out loud to get it out in the open. Monique didn't like keeping things bottled up, even if that meant talking to herself. That's why her and her sister didn't get along. Holding her tongue was not a skill that Monique possessed when it came to her personal life.

Monique pulled into a parking space and hopped out of her car. She had given herself a good pep talk on the twenty-minute drive to the restaurant. She wasn't sure why it mattered that her sister hinted at sleeping with her ex. Yes, their relationship was shit, but she would never do something so hurtful to her own flesh and blood.

Monique sighed. It was a pity that she couldn't trust her only sister. And it was sad that Ashley wanted to hold grudges, for whatever reason. But Monique was finished with the whole dysfunctional situation. It was time to let go and let God.

"Hey, Moni! I missed you, homie." Venus walked up and embraced Monique outside of the restaurant.

Monique hugged her friend tightly. She thanked God for a friend like Venus. Someone who had been with her through thick and thin, and was a ride or die true friend. Monique would never have to question if Venus was telling her the truth or not.

"Hey, V! Chiiile, let me tell you what happened when I got home this evening." Monique pulled Venus by the arm to the bar.

"Oh Lord. What in the world is going on now?" Venus' pretty face held a confused expression.

"Girl, Ashley showed up to my house talking big shit. Then she insinuated that she and Damon had something going on behind my back."

"Wait a damn minute!" Venus' voice was elevated, but she didn't seem to notice. "What the hell do you mean Ashley and Damon?"

"Just what I said. She all but said she had slept with him, but then when I told her I didn't give a damn, she tried to backtrack. You tried to tell me, and my dumb ass kept defending her because she was my sister. I feel so stupid." Monique had to swallow her pride. Venus was the last person that would judge her, so Monique had to take the time to exorcise all of the demons of her horrible relationship.

Monique relayed the story of how she threatened to beat the hell out of her sister on her front porch, and all the nasty things that she and Ashley said to one another.

"Listen, friend. We all make mistakes. Just let it go. Karma is real and she will pay for all the mess she put you through. Besides, you are way too classy to be out in the streets acting like a hood rat. You know we don't do that." Venus smirked, and Monique laughed.

Venus was right. Acting a fool was the last thing Monique needed to be caught doing. No matter how much Ashley may have deserved a good slap or two or three. Monique wouldn't be the one to give it to her. *At least not in public.*

"You're right."

"I usually am..." Venus interrupted snidely with mirth twinkling in her light brown eyes.

Just when they were looking for seats in the packed establishment, Monique's cell beeped with a notification that Nikki wasn't coming.

"Nikki's not coming. It's packed in here, so let's find somewhere else to go. I need to relax without all these people around," Monique stated.

Venus smirked. "My prayers have been answered."

Monique swatted at her friend playfully. Monique was secretly glad that Nikki wasn't coming. At least she didn't have to spend the rest of her night playing peace maker.

The two women left the lounge and headed for their vehicles. Monique was just getting settled behind the wheel when her phone rang. She almost ignored it, but something made her check the caller. It was Pearson Grant.

"Well, hello, Mr. Grant. What can I do for you?" Monique couldn't help the smile that spread across her face. She assumed Pearson was calling to discuss the good news about his approval rating going up.

"Miss Carter, I have a proposition for you."

The way Pearson purred the word *proposition* made Monique's panties wet *again.*

Well damn!

14

WHAT HAPPENS IN VEGAS...

Pearson walked swiftly up Monique's driveway. He had to stop himself from damn near running because he was so excited. It was finally his chance to get Monique away from Dallas and to a place where it would be just the two of them. Even Keifer didn't know that they were off to Vegas. Pearson was glad that Mark was back in town, so he could make sure the office continued to run smoothly. Pearson also made it a point to send Keifer to a conference in Florida, so he wouldn't be able to interrupt him and Monique. All his bases had been covered.

Pearson knocked and then rested against the door jamb as he heard rustling coming from inside. He looked around, admiring her well-kept yard. He wished he could've said he'd never seen it before, but because his obsession was out of control as it was, he'd seen various pictures of Monique's place, courtesy of Dom.

When the door swung open, it brought Pearson out of his thoughts.

Monique stood with radiant skin. Her hair was up in a messy bun and she was rocking a pair of jeans and an off the shoulder sweater. Just that little glimpse of her skin made Pearson want to lick all of her delicious flesh, starting with that beautiful smooth shoulder.

He must've been staring for too long because if he wasn't mistaken, he was certain that Monique was blushing.

"Hey. Can you help me with my bags? They're a little heavy," she requested breathlessly, making Pearson wonder if she was as turned on by the sight of him as he was with a simple look at her.

"Of course, I can." Pearson gave her his blinding, white smile as he leaned in and kissed her cheek. He took her bag and easily maneuvered it toward him.

Monique blushed again before she turned to close and lock her door. Pearson led her to the waiting car. He was determined to get Monique to not be so hesitant when it came to him. He wanted her, and if it was the last damn thing he did, he was going to get her to realize how good they could be together. He just had to tap into the charm that he'd never used.

"So I did some research on the conference. The opening luncheon and the closing dinner banquet will probably be the best place to socialize and take advantage of photo ops. Now, the keynote speaker is Jeffery Mann, and I know there's some history between the two of you, but you definitely need to be there." Monique continued to rattle off the busy itinerary, but Pearson didn't hear anything after hearing that Jeffery Mann would be at the conference.

Pearson didn't know how he missed that the old windbag would be at the conference. He was so wrapped up in all of his conspiracy theories, reputation cleanup, and getting Monique into his bed that he hadn't checked the details of the event. Jeffery Man was the last person he wanted to deal with. Pearson wanted all his focus on Monique.

They arrived at the airport in no time at all and boarded the flight. Pearson thought it was strange how comfortable it felt to travel with Monique by his side. Although his mind continued to drift back to the fact that he and Jeffery Mann were going to be in the same room after years of corporate fighting, Pearson couldn't help but be aware of Monique's every move.

When they were finally ready for take-off, Pearson was wound so tight that if he had a piece of coal, it would definitely be a diamond by the time they landed.

"You haven't said much. Is everything okay?" Monique's soft question broke into Pearson's wayward thoughts.

"Yes. I'm sorry. I have a lot on my mind." Pearson gave her a soft smile in return. He didn't want there to be tension between them, so he made a conscious effort to relax.

"You know the interview went well. There were hardly any responses about the negative interview. All anyone could talk about was how much of a hero you are. The plan worked, so all there is left to do now is lay low and stay out of trouble for a few weeks."

The smile she gave him was reassuring, and he knew that she was worried that he was concerned about the job she had done.

"I trust you, Monique. I know it was hard work in the beginning, but I trust your judgment." Pearson took her small hand in his and caressed the back of it encouragingly. "I hope you know that."

When her lips spread into a smile, Pearson couldn't help his desire to kiss her succulent lips. He licked his own lips and without another second of hesitation, he leaned in and kissed her. He felt Monique melt into him as her small hand caressed his face. The kiss was sweet and reassuring, not like the passionate one they'd shared before but just as arousing.

Pearson reluctantly pulled away and cleared his throat. He knew Monique was cautious about their budding relationship, so he would do his best not to drag her to the tiny bathroom and make her a member of the mile-high club, so he decided not to jump her bones at least while they were still on the plane.

The rest of the flight was uneventful and before he knew it, they arrived at the *Aria* hotel in Vegas. The check-in to the opulent hotel was smooth. As soon as Pearson gave his name, the concierge appeared immediately, giving his undivided attention. The tall, lanky man with silver-blond hair moved with efficiency. He had bell boys retrieve their luggage, had the room card ready, and was leading them to the private elevator in less than five minutes. Pearson admired the man's competence.

"Please, sir and madam." The concierge let them into the room with a swipe of a card. He fluttered about, turning on lights and checking the setup, and when everything was to his liking, he looked toward Pearson with a smile. "If you need anything, my name is Jean Luke. I'll be at your service for the duration of your stay." He nodded and left as quickly as he had appeared.

"Well, he certainly is efficient," Monique commented as she looked around the lavish room. Pearson had to admit he was impressed. The room was one of the biggest he'd ever seen.

"Yes, he was." Pearson's voice had deepened at the thought of having Monique in a hotel room alone *finally*.

"So this is a really nice setup." Monique walked around the living area, taking in all of what the room had to offer.

Pearson watched her closely, his eyes roaming over her body with every step she took. He had never known a woman who could hold his attention like she did. Even though she wasn't trying.

"Only the best for you," Pearson stated as he continued to watch her.

Monique nodded as she giggled.

"What's so funny?" Pearson asked, intrigued by the light sound coming from her.

"I've never had a boyfriend treat me to such lavishness, fake or otherwise." She turned and smiled at him.

"Well, that is truly shameful. And I will never give you anything less than what you deserve." Pearson knew that Monique thought they were just pretending, but it was his mission to make her see that everything between them was real.

~

PEARSON AND MONIQUE decided to go to dinner and relax before the activities began the next day. Again, the sight of Monique in her dinner attire made Pearson want to devour her whole.

The long and flowing maxi dress complemented her milk chocolate complexion. It caressed her curves delicately, and the sweetheart neckline showed just the right amount of cleavage. The simple diamond studs she wore called attention to the elegant slope of her neck. Her outfit made Pearson glad it was warm in Vegas this time of year.

"Wow! You look delicious," Pearson couldn't help but comment. She couldn't deny what was between them, and he knew she was just as attracted to him as he was to her. She just didn't want to mix business with personal.

"Thank you, Pearson," Monique replied with a smile. "You look pretty damn edible yourself."

Pearson laughed out loud. He hadn't expected her to be so blunt. The comment shocked and amused him.

"So I guess you decided to break out of that shell, huh?" Pearson said, still chuckling.

"When in Vegas..." Monique shrugged as she laughed along with him.

"Listen, we are in the party city that never sleeps, so we might as well let loose, have fun, and get to know one another in the process. Like you said on the plane, everything is going exactly how you said it would, so we can relax just a little." Pearson wanted to convince her that she could have fun with him. All she had to do was lower her inhabitations just a little.

"Okay, I can do that. But we can't do anything too crazy. We are here so that you can network and show everyone the new and improved Pearson. No asshole behavior." Monique held her hand out for Pearson to shake and he smiled. She should've known she was making a deal with the devil.

They took the elevator down to Sage, the on-site restaurant. Before they exited the elevator, Pearson grabbed Monique's hand and led her through the bustling casino. Even when the crowd thinned out, he kept her hand possessively in his.

Pearson couldn't help but notice the appreciative looks that Monique received, so he placed his hand on the small of her back and pulled her closer to his body. When she looked up at him with a question in her big doe eyes, he couldn't help but stop where they stood.

Pearson leaned down a breath away from her juicy berry-colored lips. "You have no idea what you do to me."

Monique shook her head and instead of backing away from his intended kiss, she tip-toed to get closer to him. And Pearson didn't hold back. He grabbed her by the waist, drawing her as close as she could get to his body. His free hand went to her nape, holding her in place as he tasted her lips.

Monique gasped, giving Pearson the opportunity he needed to dip his tongue into her wet mouth. Her taste was unique, a mixture of sweetness and seduction that he couldn't get enough of. Pearson was lost in the feeling of her lush breasts pressed against his chest. Her soft scent and exotic taste were intoxicating. It was as if time had stopped for them, but the world around them continued to move.

"Damn! I don't want to stop kissing you." Pearson breathed when he finally mustered up the strength to pull away from Monique's lips.

"Who said you had to stop?" Monique replied as she pecked his lips again.

Pearson groaned. He didn't know what had caused the change in Monique. Maybe it was because they were away from Dallas and in Sin City. Whatever the case, Pearson was glad Monique seemed to leave all of her reservations behind.

"This is our first *real* date. I owe you dinner, conversation, and then I will do whatever you will let me do." Pearson gave her one more lingering kiss before continuing toward the restaurant.

"How can a girl say no to that?" Monique smiled.

Again, Pearson didn't know what brought on her change of heart, but he wouldn't look a gift horse in the mouth.

"Hopefully, *no* will be the last thing you'll saying tonight." Pearson smiled wickedly.

When they arrived at the restaurant, the maître d' promptly showed them to a romantically decorated, private table in a secluded section. The table sat among flowers and candlelight with soft music playing.

"Well, you're certainly doing all the right things to make a girl say yes," Monique flirted as she sat gracefully in the chair Pearson pulled out for her.

"You have no idea what I'll do to hear you say yes," Pearson whispered seductively in Monique's ear.

Monique squirmed in her seat as he tucked her under the table. *If that can make her squirm, I can't wait to really get my hands on her.*

After they were seated and the waiter took their orders and poured them each a nice glass of wine, Pearson settled in to charm the hell out of Monique. *She won't know what hit her.*

"So tell me about yourself," Pearson stated with a wicked twinkle in his eyes. As much as he fantasized about Monique and as much time as they spent together working, she didn't talk about herself much.

Technically, he'd had Dom investigate her, so everything he knew was from that, but she hadn't told him anything personally. So that was something he was looking forward to.

Monique chuckled lightly. "A man like you has his ways of knowing all about somebody that works for him."

Pearson nodded. "Of course, I do, but I want to hear it from *you*. And you're not just somebody who *works for me*."

"So you're telling me that you want to act like this is a date, *date*?" Monique asked with curiosity written all over her beautiful face.

"This is a date, *date*," Pearson stated with authority.

"Umkay. Look, this past month and a half has been more than a little crazy for both of us, so let's just forget about the normal dating scenario and just enjoy each other's company while we're in Vegas. No expectations." Pearson held up his glass.

"I can definitely agree to that." Monique held up her glass, and with a toast, they sealed their fate.

15

GO WITH THE FLOW

P earson's wicked smiles and sweet caresses to multiple parts of her body had Monique ready to break out of her skin with eagerness. She hoped that she wasn't sending Pearson mixed signals. They had their stolen moments, and even shared a kiss or two, but Monique couldn't get over the fact that sleeping with a client was definitely a no-no. She wanted to keep her reputation intact, but she had come to the conclusion, with the help of Venus, to stop fighting her attraction to Pearson.

"*Pearson just called and asked me to go to Vegas,*" *Monique told Venus excitedly. Even though it would be a work trip, Monique was excited to get out of town. Her other clients could be handled from anywhere. And if there was immediate attention needed, Blake could handle it.*

"*Are you going to go?*" *Venus asked, her eyes bright with interest.*

"*Yes, he's my biggest client,*" *Monique responded evasively. She didn't want to admit out loud that she wanted to go to Vegas, so she could spend more time with Pearson.*

Venus waved her hand in a dismissive gesture. "Girl, bye. Pearson Grant being a client is the last thing your horny ass should be thinking about."

"Who says I'm horny?" Monique responded with her mouth gaping open in indignation.

Venus pursed her lips. "Moni, you damn near salivate when you talk about Pearson. It's not that I blame you, but you ain't foolin' nobody with this all-business act."

"It is business. You know me better than that." Monique crossed her arms over her chest.

"I know you need to get that stick out of your ass and let your hair down. You spend so much time fixing everybody else. Now, you have a chance to work on you. Have fun. Have a drink or two. Hell, have an orgasm. Just relax for once and stop thinking. Go with the flow!"

Monique decided to do just that, go with the flow. Besides, they were over a thousand miles away from home, and she was tired of not getting what she wanted. And she wanted Pearson Grant.

Monique had always walked the straight and narrow, she did everything by the book and followed her very own do's and don'ts. And it worked, at least in business, but her personal life was another story. So now it was time to do something different. *Go with the flow.*

"I really appreciate the dinner, Pearson. It was wonderful." Monique said as Pearson led her out of the restaurant his hand on the small of her back.

His large hand was spread wide over her and the heat radiating from him was giving Monique all kinds of naughty ideas. His tall muscular frame was draped in a slim cut black suit, and a coal black dress shirt with the top few buttons undone, and a light blue pocket square. His golden blond hair was swept back from his face, and his bright eyes were alight with mischief, seduction, and lust.

"Dinner was just the beginning. Stick with me, kid and I'll show you how to properly *do* Vegas." Pearson winked, and Monique swooned like a teen.

Pearson grabbed her hand, and again led her through the casino. It felt so natural to be with him like this. As a matter of fact, even traveling with him felt natural. It felt as if they were a couple. Maybe, she was thinking to deeply into a fling, but Monique couldn't help the connection she felt with Pearson.

"I see we're not going back to the suite, so what's the plan for the night?" Monique asked with a mixture of excitement and curiosity as they walked through a pair of double doors.

"Oh, you will see." Pearson helped her into a waiting limo and smoothly slid in beside her.

The car pulled away from the curb and into traffic, an array of lights and sounds surrounded them. Monique felt positively giddy. The rush of adrenaline she got from stepping outside of her normal routine caused her to feel almost high.

When the limo rolled to a stop outside a nondescript building, Monique quirked a brow at Pearson in question. When he just smirked, she knew that he wouldn't divulge what was going on unless she asked him directly.

"Where are we? And don't tell me I'll see. I'm not really one who likes surprises." Monique continued to study the building trying to find any distinguishing markings, but the only thing she saw was a statue of a pair of legs wearing fishnet stockings and high heeled shoes. *I know he didn't bring me to a strip club.*

"Relax, sweetheart. I promise not to take you anywhere that you would feel uncomfortable. This is just the back entrance to the Crazy Horse Burlesque Show. I'm not famous or anything, but I know a guy." Pearson smiled and Monique relaxed. *Okay, so classy strippers. At least I don't need any dollar bills.*

She was all for relaxing and going with the flow, but she knew she wasn't ready for lap dances any time soon.

"I can see on your face that you think this is some tawdry night full of dollar bills and sweat, but I promise it's a really good show."

"Okay, I'll take your word for it." Monique couldn't help but laugh at how spot on he was in what she was thinking. She had only been to Vegas once before, and unfortunately she didn't get a chance to catch a show. So once again she would have to remind herself to keep an open mind and chill.

The driver stepped out and opened the limo door, and Pearson slid out and took her hand in his. As soon as she stepped out of the car, he tucked her closely to his side. Monique couldn't help but feel protected, and oddly, turned on.

She wouldn't dare compare her two-year relationship with Damon to the one day her and Pearson had decided to be romantic, but it already felt different. Damon never grabbed her hand, or tucked her protectively against him. He always made her feel like she was clingy if she wanted that. Monique shook her head, the last thing she wanted to do was think about her ex when she was supposed to be having fun.

The inside of the theater wasn't what she'd expected. Everything from the walls to the floors were dripping in red velvet. The tables, chairs, even the lamps were all red. The lighting was low and the music was hypnotizing. The sophisticated hostess with a severe bun showed them to a booth that was center stage but on a raised podium in the back. Of course, the seats were the best in the house.

Monique was excited and the glass of champagne she sipped made her feel dizzy. Pearson although sitting right next to her, wasn't touching her like before. She couldn't help but feel like he was teasing her somehow.

Once the houselights went down, and the music turned up, Monique did her best to focus on the show. And what a show it was! It was like nothing she had ever seen before. Yes, the women were topless, but the show was so mesmerizingly entertaining that Monique forgot all about their nudity. The women were all the same height and build, and even though they were all different races, they looked like clones. Their movements were intricate, sharp, graceful, and so very seductive that Monique wriggled in her seat.

Out of all the things she had expected, becoming aroused had *not* been one of them. The glistening bodies of the long-legged dancers twirling and writhing seductively around the stage had Monique almost panting. Pearson was so close that she could feel the heat radiating from his body, and it was making her girly parts sit up and take notice.

When there was an intermission, Monique had to excuse herself to the ladies' room to freshen up. Even though he had still yet to touch her, she needed to get herself together before she mounted Pearson and rode him like the stallion she imagined him to be.

Upon entering the posh restroom, she had to admire the décor. The sexy theme from the show was evident even in the restroom. It had a red chaise lounge with red and gold chandeliers, and lamps throughout the separate sitting room. The actual restroom was through another set of doors.

"Well, isn't this fancy." Monique said out loud as she checked out the space.

She headed to the vanity mirror that was set-up by the chaise and sat down to reapply her lipstick when she heard the door open. Monique continued to primp in the mirror not paying attention to who entered.

"You look beautiful." The deep voice scared her and Monique whipped around, and jumped up with her hand on her chest.

"Pearson what the hell? You can't be in here. What if someone saw you?" Monique looked around frantically to make sure they were alone.

Pearson had the nerve to chuckle. No matter how much she told herself to relax, she couldn't get out of work mode. Even though they weren't in Dallas, if anyone saw Pearson Grant in the ladies' restroom, it still could potentially be a scandal.

"Nobody saw me. I just wanted to check and make sure you were okay. You looked a little flushed when you left our table."

The nerve. He could've at least pretended not to see my horniness. But out loud Monique replied simply, "I'm fine."

"Great." Pearson stalked toward her like a panther, lethal and calculating. Monique clenched her legs together tight to try to ward off the throbbing sensation in her pussy. It felt like every time they were in a room together; she would melt into a pile of hormones.

"You don't mind if I check to make sure." Pearson was right in front of her, his minty breath mingling with hers.

"Che... check? How exactly are you going to check?" Monique stammered.

Pearson leaned down and kissed her stammering lips softly. His touch was a contradiction to his words, and it confused Monique. However, before she could question him again, he stroked his fingers over her puckered nipples.

The thin material of her dress did nothing to hide the fact that she was completely enamored with the man, and he took every advantage. Pearson continued to kiss her slowly as he plucked and tugged her sensitive buds.

"Damn, you feel so good, gorgeous. I want to fuck you so bad right now." Pearson moved his hand to her ass and squeezed. His other hand continued to roll her nipples back and forth. The pleasure mixed with the small bite of pain had her panting with arousal.

Monique had never experienced an orgasm from just her breasts being touched, but she had a glorious feeling this would be her first time.

Monique pressed her body up against his again, every time they were close she couldn't help but feel like a feline, rubbing up against him marking her territory. However, she still couldn't help herself, so when she moaned out loud and begged Pearson to fuck her, she couldn't say that she was shocked. Hell, all of her inhibitions were out the door.

But he didn't fuck her. He continued to sweetly torture her nipples until she was a quivering shaking mess wrapped in his muscular arms.

Once she had gathered her composure, Pearson released her, tucked her breasts back into her dress and kissed the top of her head.

"Give me your panties," he said with a straight face, but Monique just knew he had to be joking.

"Uh, no thank you," Monique responded. He had just rubbed her to orgasm without so much as grazing her vagina, but that didn't stop her from soaking through the little black thong that she had on. So there wasn't any way in hell that she was about to strip off her drenched underwear, and give them to him.

Pearson chuckled darkly, and Monique knew that she was messed up because the shit turned her on even more. "Oh, sweet beautiful one, that was *not* a question. Give. Me. Your. Panties."

Monique backed away from him, and he released her. She really didn't know if she wanted to go down this rabbit hole. If she played this seductive game, could she walk away when it was over? Could she be his next "companion" and still have her dignity intact?

Go with the flow.

Monique nodded, gathered up her long dress in one hand, and with the other hand she hooked her fingers in her panties and slid them down her legs. She stepped out of them one leg at a time and held the wet material in her hand.

She was a grown woman. A sensual grown woman and she could have a tryst in Sin City if she wanted to. Monique took a deep breath, and thrusts the panties forward before she changed her mind. She could talk big all day long, but it was another thing doing it big.

Pearson took the panties from her grasp, and raised them to his nose. He inhaled deeply then placed them in his pocket with a sinister smile covering his handsome face. The look made Monique's blood burn with lust.

"If your dress was shorter, I would eat your pussy right now because you smell so delicious. But I can wait. Let's go back to our seats before we miss the rest of the show."

Pearson leaned down and kissed Monique's lips sweetly like he didn't just blow her damn mind with his raunchy display and filthy words. The man was too many things all at once, and Monique couldn't say that she didn't get a thrill from it.

16

WHEN OPPORTUNITY KNOCKS

Pearson had so many plans for Monique, but he had to sit through the rest of the burlesque show before he could put them into motion. The first half of the show had been pure torture. She'd sat prettily in her low-cut dress, looking like a Grecian goddess. And to make sure he didn't do anything inappropriate, he'd kept his hands to himself.

Touching her skin was an aphrodisiac, and once he started, he couldn't possibly stop. He wanted to see her beautiful face brighten, her pouty lips purse, and her chest heave in anticipation. He wanted to see that desire that he knew she hid deep down inside. Pearson wanted her to lose her inhibitions and give in to the lust between the two of them. And tonight, he was going to make that happen.

Although he kept his hands to himself, his attention stayed on Monique. He could tell that she was fighting her arousal, and he wanted to do something about it. When Monique excused herself to the restroom, he could see that her nipples were pebbled through the top of her dress, and he knew without any doubt that he had to touch her. And there was no way he could wait a moment longer.

Pearson followed her to the restroom at a leisurely pace. He wanted to give her time to get comfortable before he made his move, he also wanted to make sure that they had the restroom all to themselves. He entered the spacious restroom and locked the door. He hoped that nobody was beyond the second set of double doors. But he didn't have the inclination to care.

When Pearson's eyes landed on Monique reapplying her lipstick, he lost all control. Her lips did something to him, and he had to admit she was one of the most beautiful women that he ever had the pleasure of seeing. His strides were long as he made his way to her.

"Pearson, what are you doing in here?" Monique gasped in shock.

"I just came to check on you." He replied smoothly with a smirk covering his lips.

Pearson leaned down and took her plump lips in a passion filled kiss. He only wanted to kiss the lipstick that she'd just applied off her lips. But when he got a taste, he couldn't stop himself. He had an overwhelming need to touch her all over.

Pearson reached inside of her dress, he caressed her breast. The feel of her hard little nub against his fingers made him want to rip off her clothes and fuck her silly. Instead, he rubbed her hardened tip as she moaned out her pleasure and begged for him not to stop. He tweaked her nipples as he devoured her sweet mouth.

When she yelled out her completion, he kissed her lips tenderly and pulled his heated hand from her dress.

"I'll wait for you outside." Pearson kissed Monique's flushed cheek as he sauntered out of the restroom.

He would postpone his orgasm until later. It was the most unselfish thing he could remember doing in a very long time. And he was definitely paying the price because his dick could hammer nails.

When Monique finally slid into the booth, her face was still flushed with lust. Pearson wanted nothing more than to pull her out the door and do the nastiest things to her. However, the lights once again dimmed, signaling for the start of the show.

Pearson decided he would have a little fun, so he slid closer to her putting his arm around the back of the booth.

"I want you to pull up your dress and open your legs," Pearson whispered in Monique's ear. It wasn't about pushing boundaries or even testing limits anymore. It was about being in the moment and taking the opportunity to actually be with someone who cared about more than herself. It was about giving pleasure when before... all he did was take it.

"Pearson, we can't do this here," Monique whispered her wide eyes betraying the lust she was so obviously feeling.

"We can and we will. Now, open those sexy legs for me." Pearson's free hand roamed up her thigh pushing the fabric upward.

Monique did as he'd asked, and he maneuvered just enough to be able to touch heaven. He slid his thick finger through her slick warmth and caressed the hardened bud that peeked out from her wet folds.

Pearson rubbed in time with the seductive beat of the music. He didn't speed up although when Monique's hips began to sway from side to side, he wanted to, but he didn't.

He knew she was getting close to an orgasm when she held her breath. The same thing had happened in the restroom when she came, and although he wanted nothing more than to see the pure unadulterated pleasure written all over her gorgeous face, he would refrain.

Pearson stopped his movement cold. When Monique quickly turned her head toward him and narrowed her eyes, Pearson simply winked and put his finger in his mouth. Monique gasped at the action and Pearson couldn't help the chuckle that slipped out.

This is going to be so much fun.

Pearson knew that Monique was more than a little tightly wound, but he thought it was just at work. It turned out that she was just as uptight outside of work as well. He knew by the time they left Vegas, Monique would be a different woman.

"What kind of game are you playing?" Monique whispered, her eyes squinted in anger.

"I promise you that this isn't a game. I just want you to enjoy the rest of the show without any distractions." Pearson leaned over and took her lips once again in a kiss. He could admit that her kisses were more addictive than he'd ever thought they could be.

"How am I supposed to watch the show? It's a little uncomfortable sitting in a puddle." Monique sassed, and Pearson groaned.

She was going to kill him. He really wasn't trying to tease her, but he couldn't watch her cum again. If she did, all of his self-control would be nonexistent. And although he was virtually unknown in Vegas, a man fucking a woman in the middle of a show would draw attention.

"Drink some more champagne, and I promise to make you cum as many times as you want, later."

Monique sighed. "You always promise me later. I suggest you take the opportunity while it's right here in front of you."

Pearson thought about her words, and she was absolutely right. He had been obsessively lusting after Monique since the day he'd met her, and now that they were finally alone, he was making her wait for what she clearly wanted, hell, what he clearly wanted.

Pearson wouldn't let this chance to be with her pass him by. But he definitely wouldn't rush. He wanted to take his time and fulfill her every desire and he would do as she suggested and take the opportunity... right now.

PEARSON DIDN'T MISS the smile that broke out on Monique's face as he placed his hand back under her dress. He would make her cum, and he would suffer the consequences until he could get her alone.

Her tight heat surrounded his finger as he dipped it in over and over again. Pearson could tell that she was trying to muffle her moans, but she was getting louder with each stroke of his hand. He leaned over and took her mouth because he didn't want anyone else to hear her cries of ecstasy. Pearson was selfish like that. He would make his woman cum anywhere she wanted, but he hated that another man could possibly see it.

Again, he had to question what he really wanted from Monique. He had never been the jealous type, so the feeling was new.

Monique's tensing legs and low groan signaled her orgasm. Pearson kissed her more deeply to continue to catch her moans.

"Oh my goodness. I-I have never..." Monique's words trailed off with a look of bewilderment.

Pearson simply nodded pulled her snuggly into his side and kissed the top of her head. "The night is still young, pretty lady. Trust this will be a night that you will never forget."

"I believe you." Monique sighed, grabbing her glass of champagne and taking a healthy gulp.

Once the show ended, Monique excused herself to the restroom again. This time, Pearson didn't follow her inside, even though he really, *really* wanted to.

When she emerged looking refreshed and glowing, Pearson simply smiled. He would do everything to keep that look of pure relaxation on her face.

The rest of the night, Pearson did things that he hadn't done in years. They did a tour of Vegas on a quirky bus full of strangers, they walked the strip and took pictures with street performers, and they danced the night away, moving from club to club.

Monique even insisted that they stop at the little white chapel and get souvenirs. They stood in front of an Elvis impersonator and laughed their way through a ceremony. Monique said that her best friend would flip when she sent her the video. She even suggested they send it to Keifer to ruffle his feathers too. She just wanted to show her friend that she could take the stick out her ass, and Pearson couldn't help but laugh in agreement.

Pearson liked the lighthearted banter between the two of them. He hadn't acted so silly and carefree in years. He realized that this just wasn't about getting her into bed anymore, or using her to fix his fucked up reputation. This was about living.

Pearson had accomplished so much, and he could admit that he was an asshole because he was unhappy. There were many reasons why, but in this moment he chose to be happy.

When they finally made it back to their suite, they were still laughing and joking. Pearson couldn't remember the last time he had laughed so much.

"Well, wife, this has been quite an evening." Pearson laughed as he sat down on the comfortable sofa in the vast living room.

Monique giggled. "Yes, husband, it has."

When Monique had texted her friend that she relaxed so much that she'd let Elvis marry her, her friend had lost her shit. Monique had to call her and calm her down, reassuring her that it was a joke and they didn't really get married.

From her friend's reaction, Pearson was glad he didn't send anything to Keifer. *I'm sure his reaction would've been much worse. Especially since Monique doesn't seem to understand just exactly what we did.*

"I'm tired and I know we have a long day tomorrow, but I really don't want this night to end." Monique sighed as she sat down next to him cuddling into his side.

It was such a natural thing for her to do that Pearson didn't question why he felt so content. He just pulled her closer.

"I'm glad you had fun. Let's go to bed."

"Together?" Monique raised her head from his shoulder and looked up at him.

"Together." Pearson smiled.

Pearson rose from the couch and tugged Monique up with him. He led her to his bedroom where he stripped off her dress, leaving her naked. He undressed himself and pulled her into the bathroom where he turned on the shower.

Monique didn't ask any questions or say anything. She just followed his lead, pulling her hair into a bun at the top of her head. They washed each other gingerly, taking in the sight of their naked bodies for the first time.

Pearson had known Monique was a beautiful woman, but he couldn't imagine just how glorious her body actually was. His manhood hardened with each swipe of his hands over her soapy body. He couldn't contain his desires any longer.

"I need you." His voice was a hoarse whisper, and he saw the shiver run through Monique.

"Then have me." With her words, Pearson no longer felt the need to hold back. He pushed her against the wall of the shower, lifted her in his muscular arms, and kissed her deeply.

When Monique instinctively wrapped her legs around his waist, Pearson didn't think. He thrust deeply into her waiting heat. Their collective moans reverberated off the walls of the shower.

It was as if something had snapped within him, and before he knew it, he was pounding into her pussy like a man possessed. Her nails bit into his shoulders as she held on to him for dear life.

"Next time, I'll take it slow, beautiful. I just... I can't right now. You just feel so fucking perfect." Monique moaned in response, and Pearson continued to plow into her willing body.

He stroked in and out, hitting her G-spot on every thrust. Pearson sucked on her neck, making sure he left a mark. He wanted to claim her as his like the animal he was. He didn't want any other man to have her.

"Yes. Oh damn. That feels so good," Monique moaned passionately.

"Take this cock. Does it feel good, baby?"

"Yes! Oh fuck, yes! I'm going to cum. Please... Just..." Pearson knew what she needed. He had already made her cum twice that night.

"Cum for me, baby. Let it go and let me feel you." Pearson put enough distance between them to rub her clit. He rubbed in time with his thrusting hips.

Monique's legs began to tighten around his waist, and she began to shake with her release. When Pearson felt the rush of wetness over his cock, he exploded. Pearson pushed his pulsating cock deep inside her quivering pussy as he moaned his release in ecstasy.

Pearson wanted to feel embarrassed at how fast he came, but the feel of her tight pussy wrapped around him would make any man lose it.

"Umm. What's the point in making me shower if you were just going to get me all dirty again?" Monique's husky voice broke through their heavy breathing.

Pearson chuckled and shook his head. "Please believe me, beautiful, I would love to keep you dirty, but we need our rest."

Monique pouted and Pearson couldn't help but kiss her one more time. When she moaned and wrapped her arms around his neck, his cock grew to stone.

"Fuck! You're going to regret teasing me, woman."

They stayed in the shower making love for another forty minutes before finally going to bed.

17

UNEXPECTED

Monique woke with a smile on her face. The previous night was not what she'd expected at all. The fun she had hanging out with Pearson was surprising to say the least. If anyone was watching them, they would have thought that they were just two drunk tourists having a good time. But neither of them was drunk. They'd only had a few drinks with dinner and at the show, but after that, they were just drunk off each other.

It was nice to just laugh, joke, and kid around without worrying about who was watching, and what people might say. It was a nice break from the reality that they lived. Monique chuckled at the memory of them laughing with Elvis while they said "I do." Venus had flipped the hell out when she thought they were actually married.

It was the best form of revenge that Monique could get. Her best friend telling her she needed to get the stick out of her ass, and then when she did, Venus freaked out about it. It was a bit extreme pretending to get married to prove a point. Monique shrugged. *It was so worth it.*

When she decided to relax, she went all out, but she didn't think she would relax right out of her panties. Admitting to herself that she'd wanted Pearson beyond logic was hard for her at first. She was the problem solver, the responsible one, and the cautious one. Being with Pearson had gone against everything she stood for professionally. But last night she didn't care.

Pearson groaned when Monique wiggled to adjust her position. She was plastered on top of his hard, muscular chest, and it was the most comfortable she had felt in months or hell, maybe even in years.

"Unless you want me to fuck you back to sleep, you better be still." Pearson's sleepy eyes peered down at her with a smirk on his lips.

The man was pure, walking, talking sex, and Monique wanted oh so badly for him to fuck her back to sleep. However, they needed to get up for the welcome luncheon for the conference.

"As much as I would like for you to do exactly that, we need to get up. It's already ten thirty, and you need to be at the luncheon in an hour." Monique reluctantly sat up from her comfortable position on his chest.

However, before she could completely dislodge herself from him, Pearson wrapped his muscular arm around her small waist and pulled her back into bed. He quickly moved on top of her and began to kiss and nuzzle her neck.

It was like her legs had a mind of their own and just fell open to accommodate the width of his body. He grinded his hard dick into her; making her pussy pulse with need, and then he easily slipped inside her. The feeling of him sliding into her felt so good, better than anything she had ever felt before, and then it hit her. *Shit, he's bare.*

"Oh my God! Pearson, stop. Stop!" Monique was frantic. She had never gone without using protection.

Pearson immediately stopped moving, but he didn't pull out. "What? What? Am I hurting you? Shit, sweetheart, I'm so sorry. I didn't mean to hurt you."

"No." Monique shook her head. "You're not wearing a condom," she said, worry dripping from her every word.

"Oh my goodness! You came in me last night. Oh shit! How could

I be so stupid?" Monique pushed at his shoulders, and Pearson finally pulled out of her and moved to her side.

"Beautiful, calm down. I know we got carried away last night, but I promise you I'm clean." Pearson grabbed her hand, and kissed it.

Monique relaxed a little at his words, but there was still the fact that what they did could result in more than a STD.

"Are you on the pill?" Pearson's words were hesitant, but he had a right to ask. Monique was pretty sure that he didn't need a fling resulting in an unwanted pregnancy.

"I'm take the shot. We should be fine. I just... I'm paranoid about safe sex." Monique relaxed a little more, but she still couldn't believe how stupid she had behaved.

"Come here, sweetheart." Pearson pulled her until she was straddling his lap. He groaned and she started to move, but he held her in place.

"That's how we got in this mess in the first place." Monique arched a brow at him, and he just smiled and placed his hands up in a surrendering motion.

"I promise to behave."

"Okay. I just freaked out a little. Sorry." Monique sighed. Their fun light-hearted morning turned sour so quickly, it made her head spin. And it was her fault. She wasn't some care-free, go with the flow type person. She was a plan and execute type of girl.

"It's okay, sweetheart. I know it's hard for you to relax. Like I said, we just got carried away. I'll use a condom until we decide to have babies." Pearson smirked, and Monique pursed her lips.

"That shit is *not* funny." Monique slapped his chest.

"Oh, come on. It was a little funny." Pearson smiled, his charm in full effect, and Monique wondered where in the world this Pearson was a few weeks back.

"If we're going to do this, Pearson, we have to use protection. No more slip ups." Monique had to make sure that he knew she was serious. All joking aside, she knew that even being on the shot wasn't a one hundred percent guarantee from unwanted pregnancies and the last thing she needed right now was a baby.

"No more slip ups. Scouts honor." Pearson held up two fingers in a scout salute and Monique rolled her eyes.

"Were you even a scout?"

"That's beside the point. You can trust me, gorgeous. I wouldn't do anything to hurt you."

Monique wanted desperately to believe him, but she knew that Pearson somehow hurting her was inevitable, because she was already falling for the tyrant that believed in companions and not relationships.

Geez, Moni, how the hell did you get yourself into this?

PEARSON HAD TALKED Monique into going to the luncheon with him. There really wasn't a need for her to go, but she was there to work first and foremost, so she'd agreed.

It was the proverbial who's who of the technology world, and she was glad that Pearson decided to come. It would be great for his image and his business. Although since the interview of him in the hospital aired, there hadn't been anymore talk of him being a reckless CEO.

Monique knew that her job would be coming to an end, and she was both glad and sad about it. If her plan worked to the degree in which she designed it, he wouldn't need her services for much longer. And that would mean that seeing him almost every day would come to an end.

But has our time together changed everything? Will he still want to carry on with this... whatever it is when I'm no longer his fixer? Will I be just another notch on his bedpost?

"This is my wife, Monique." Pearson's deep voice brought Monique out of her disparaging thoughts, A second later, his words registered.

Why the hell is he introducing me as his wife?

"Hi, it's nice to meet you." Monique smiled politely at the man whose name she didn't catch. She was a professional and kept a cool demeanor even though Pearson had surprised her with his introduction.

"And it's nice to meet you as well. So what made a beautiful woman like you marry someone as callous as Grant here?" the man asked arrogantly, a smile on his thin, pink lips.

Monique had a feeling that his little remark was supposed to be some sort of joke, but for some reason, it rubbed her the wrong way.

"I don't know about callous, but he is quite the charmer." She smiled sweetly and looked up at Pearson and winked. Monique could tell by his rigid stance that he didn't really care for the man or at least, his comments. So she decided to do what she did best—fix it.

"Oh my, can you please excuse us? My sorority sister just walked in and she's been dying to meet my Pear. It was great to meet you," Monique threw over her shoulder as she pulled Pearson in the opposite direction.

When they were far enough away, Monique stopped and turned to a smirking Pearson.

"What?" she asked, confused by his smirk.

"Do you honestly think he believed you saw your sorority sister here?"

"I could have seen anyone here," Monique said with an exaggerated eye roll. "Besides, it got us away from that guy."

"Yeah, he's a real ass. And normally I would've put him in his place, but you're the one that said no asshole behavior. I was just following orders."

"Well, I like it when you follow orders." Monique's voice was husky as she licked her lips and Pearson's eyes narrowed on the motion of her tongue. She knew that she was playing with fire. But for some reason she couldn't help herself.

Pearson made her feel wanted, and sexy. He looked at her like she was the most desirable woman in the room, hell, the planet. She wanted him to want her because she wanted the hell out of him.

"Mrs. Grant..." Pearson took a step in her direction. "Just because we are in public that will not stop me from fucking you," Pearson continued with a low growl into her ear.

Monique gasped. She definitely had to get used to Pearson's dirty mouth. The nasty things he said to her made her nipples hard and her pussy pulse. The effect he had on her body was ridiculous.

"We are in public, surrounded by your peers. You cannot talk about *effing* me," Monique whispered, as she looked around. She hoped that nobody had heard their conversation, but nobody seemed to be paying them any attention, so Monique calmed down a little.

"I told you last night, wife, I will do you anywhere I please." Pearson held his serious face, and Monique knew that she had pushed some imaginary button that had set off the beast.

"Okay, *husband*. Just relax. Like I told you last night, you can do whatever you want to me in private." Monique thought it was cute that his little nickname for her was wife after their fake ceremony, and it seemed to calm him down when she called him husband. *Whatever floats your boat, Cowboy.* Monique shook her head at the strangeness of the situation.

Pearson was a walking contradiction. Claiming only to have "situationships" that he virtually controlled, and now he was staking his claim by calling her wife to anyone that would listen. *So weird.*

"Let's go somewhere private then. You didn't let me finish this morning." Pearson moved closer to her, and her world tilted just a little.

The sweet smell of his cologne and the way his eyes shined down at her made her want to drag him off and let him do whatever the hell he wanted. However, Monique knew that at least one of them had to have some kind of self-control. So she took a deep breath and told him no.

"You have some work to do, sir. We can have alone time later." She tiptoed to kiss the side of his mouth and grabbed his hand. "Let's find our table. The ceremony is about to begin."

"Don't think I'm not going to collect later. You owe me, sweetheart. And I always collect on my debts." Pearson winked at her and she felt her face heat.

Monique knew that he was a man of his word and she couldn't wait until he collected. *Forgive me for being such a sinner in sin city.*

Monique led them to their designated table, and Pearson pulled out the chair for her. She sat down and smiled up at him.

"Ever the gentlemen." Monique winked, and Pearson chuckled.

"Anything for you, wife." Pearson kissed her lips and took his seat.

"Aren't you two just adorable?" an older woman with graying blond hair and a bright smile asked. "How long have you been married. I can sense that you are newlyweds. It's the joy in your faces."

"No, ma'am, we're not actually..." Monique didn't get to finish her sentence because the last person on earth that she thought she would see in Vegas was marching toward her.

"What the hell are you doing here? And with *him* of all people?"

"Damon? What are you doing here?" Monique hadn't seen or heard from him since she ghosted his cheating ass more than a month before.

"I'm an engineer at a technology firm. What the hell do you think I'm doing here?" He sneered hatefully.

Monique could see that he was about to cause a scene, and that was the last thing that she wanted. Pearson was doing so great, and she didn't want to be the cause of any negativity coming his way.

"You need to lower your voice. You are starting to gain attention," Monique whispered smiling nervously at the older couple at their table.

Damon lowered his voice, but the hateful words continued. "You're taking trips with him now? That's how you act as soon as you leave me?"

Monique was baffled. Why did he act like he wasn't the one cheating on her? *The audacity.*

"You need to watch how the fuck you talk to my wife," Pearson growled.

"*Wife?*" Damon whipped his head toward Monique, giving her the death glare.

"Pearson, you are not helping!" Monique had to get this under control before it all went tits up.

"Beautiful, relax. I got this." Pearson stood from his chair, and

Monique quickly did the same. She wasn't big enough to break up a fight and she wasn't crazy enough to try. So she began to walk toward the exit.

"Outside now," Monique said through clenched teeth at the man who somehow thought a fake wedding meant a real wife.

18

TILL DEATH DO US PART

Pearson dutifully followed a seething Monique, but not because she was angry. It was because *he* was. Pearson didn't know why this Damon character thought he could talk to Monique any kind of way, but he was about to put a stop to that bullshit immediately.

Damon had had his chance and he'd blown it. That was one thing that Pearson would not do. He would make sure that Monique knew exactly how he felt about her. Last night had changed everything, and little did Monique know, this was more than some fling. She was his now, so she had better get used to it.

Pearson was deep in thought when Damon's harsh words brought him to an abrupt stop. Pearson inhaled deeply to calm himself down. He didn't want to ruin everything that Monique had worked so hard for. *I won't kick his ass. I won't kick his ass,* Pearson chanted over and over again in his head.

"Why is he calling you his wife, Monique?" Damon sneered and Pearson stepped forward before Monique put a hand on his chest.

I swear I'm going to kick his ass, I. Am. Going. To. Kick. His. Ass!

"You don't get to ask me questions, Damon!" Monique pursed her lips at him.

"That's complete bullshit, Monique! What the hell are you doing?" Damon shook his head, his dreads moving from side to side with the motion.

"I don't have to explain anything to you!" Monique's teeth were clenched and Pearson could see her temper written all over her face. Her normally chocolate complexion held undertones of red, and she looked like she was going to blow at any moment.

"Pshh. I never thought you would be the type to sleep your way to the top. Is this how you dealt with all of your so-called clients?" Damon asked sarcastically. Pearson could see that his hateful words were hitting their mark. Monique looked positively heartbroken.

"Listen, man, you really need to watch your fucking mouth. Do you think I won't beat the fuck out of you?" Pearson's thin patience was nonexistent and he knew Monique would be more than a little pissed when he slugged the asshole. *This motherfucker has it coming!*

"Who the fuck do you think you are?" Damon turned his glare on Pearson.

"I already told you who the fuck I am!" Pearson's face blazed with fury and there wouldn't be anything that would be able to calm him down if he got a hold of this jerk.

"Okay. That's enough." Monique stomped her foot. "I will not have you two causing a scene. Everyone has too much to lose, and cursing, yelling, and acting a fool at this prestigious conference is not a good look."

Pearson was properly chastised, but he still wanted to beat the shit out of Damon.

"Damon, we have nothing to say to one another. *Nothing!*" Pearson could see the fire coming out of her, and his dick hardened at the sight.

"We have a lot to say, Monique. I can't believe you would treat me this way. After all this time." The bite was gone out of Damon's voice as he pleaded. Pearson saw the shift in the other man's demeanor, and he knew Damon was about to start begging. Pearson could tell the asshole was a master manipulator.

"Monique, I'm sorry, beautiful. I didn't mean to upset you,"

Pearson interrupted before Damon really started to grovel. "But we need to go back to the luncheon." *I'll be damned if he uses Monique's soft heart to get his way.*

"You're right, Pearson. We're here to *work*. This is nonsense. Let's go." Monique stormed away, and Pearson couldn't help but watch her leave.

Damn, that ass.

"This shit ain't over." Damon snarled at Pearson.

"Yes, the fuck it is," Pearson threw over his shoulder as he sauntered after Monique.

Pearson caught up to her before she entered the ballroom and pulled her into a deserted hallway.

"Hey. Slow down." Pearson pulled Monique into his arms and embraced her warmly. "Are you alright?"

Monique sighed. "Yeah. I'm fine. I can't believe after all these weeks, he shows up here of all places." She shook her head making her curls swing against her shoulders as she looked away.

"Look at me, sweetheart." Pearson placed his fingers under Monique's chin, and made her look at him. Her brown eyes were watery with unshed tears, and it pissed him off.

How dare some asshole make his woman cry. They were having a great time, and now he would bet his last nickel that she was second guessing everything.

"That guy isn't worth a damn and he certainly ain't worth your tears." Pearson hugged her tighter leaning down to kiss her on her forehead.

"I just work so hard and now, just like I knew would happen because I'm with you, people are going to accuse me of sleeping my way to success." The tears slipped down Monique's cheeks, making Pearson sorry that he hadn't pummeled the jerk when he had the chance.

"Fuck what other people think! You are damn good at your job. Look at me. I've been to more charity events in the last month than I have my entire career." Pearson said sincerely.

"You've made me want to be better. Hell, you've made me better.

My horrible reputation was earned, and you turned everything around in just a few months. Don't you ever let anyone take that away from you. Do you hear me?"

Monique nodded at him with a small smile playing on her glossy lips. Pearson kissed her because he couldn't look at her another second without touching her intimately. He hated to see her sad, and especially because of her cheating bastard of an ex. Damon definitely didn't deserve her, and he sure as fuck didn't deserve to be able to break her heart.

Monique took a deep breath, took a Kleenex from the pocket of her dress, and wiped her face. Pearson could see she was carefully gathering her composure. *Always the consummate professional.*

"Okay. I'm good. Let's go network."

Pearson kissed her lips once more. "That's my girl."

THE REST of the luncheon was monotonous, and Pearson's patience had been used trying not to fight Damon, so he talked Monique into leaving. He wanted to have more time to spend with her just relaxing and enjoying each other like they did the night before.

Besides, this trip was to get away from all the craziness that was going on back in Dallas, although Monique didn't actually know that. She thought they were actually there to work. Pearson couldn't care less about the convention. He didn't really give a damn what those people thought about him, even though his presence seemed to be helping his reputation.

Monique had decided to go into her bedroom to get some work done for a client, so Pearson took the opportunity to call Dom to see if he had found any more information about his hit and run accident.

"Grant, how's Vegas treating you?" Dom answered his phone on the first ring.

"Vegas has been unexpected," Pearson responded with a smirk.

"Uh huh. What the hell were you thinking, Grant? And how in the world did you get Monique to agree to that?" Dom asked, his deep voice rumbling over the line his displeasure could be heard loud and clear. Pearson should've known that Dom would know exactly what he was up to, even if he was thousands of miles away.

"Hey, it wasn't me. I went along with what she wanted," Pearson defended.

"That's hard for me to believe. I've known you over half our lives. Once you want something, there's no stopping you, so what the fuck man?"

"I have it under control. I swear. Just let me handle this, and you relax. Now. Let's get down to the reason I called." Pearson changed the subject. He didn't particularly like the judgmental tone his friend was using with him.

"Alright. Just make sure you handle it. Because if you don't, the explosion could be detrimental," Dom said, and Pearson could imagine he was shaking his head.

"Yeah. Dude, I got it. Now, did you find anything on the driver?" Pearson asked.

Dom sighed loudly but dropped the subject, "Yeah the vehicle was stolen of course. I tracked down the owner, and where the car was stolen from. It looks like the car had only been missing for a few hours at the time of your hit and run."

"So, I was right? Somebody is targeting me?" Pearson ran his hand up and down the back of his neck.

"I haven't crossed that off my list of possibilities," Dom responded evading the question.

Pearson really hated when he did that shit. Dom was always so cautious when it came to an investigation, but that's what made him so damn good at what he did.

"Okay, so, what other possibilities are there?" Pearson asked frustrated.

"Joy rider, drug addict, or driving while texting. There is an array of possibilities of why somebody could've hit you then kept going."

"But you don't honestly believe any of those?" Pearson asked, but he knew Dom didn't think any of those things was the real reason he was nearly killed on the side of the road.

"No. The car was ditched soon after. My guys are running the prints now to see if there are any matches."

"Shit. Do you think I'm being paranoid?" Pearson asked his long-time friend. Maybe he was just at the wrong place at the wrong time.

"Honestly. No. I think that somebody got lucky when you stopped to help that woman. It was the opportunity they needed to cause you harm and make it look like an accident. Nobody is that damn distracted that they plow into a car without slamming on the brakes."

Finally, Pearson thought. He knew that he heard the car speed up. He wasn't crazy.

"At least I know I'm not paranoid. Somebody's just trying to kill me," Pearson said dryly. He was relieved that he wasn't irrational, but now he would be even more suspicious. Because now it wasn't just him he would be worried about, it was Monique.

He had to make sure and protect her from whatever threats there were against him, because he was entirely too selfish to let her go.

"Just stay in Vegas, and let me worry about the shit show that's going on here. If things change, I'll let you know." Dom disconnected the call before Pearson had a chance to thank him.

Dom was a good friend, and as close as a brother that Pearson would ever have. But he had to wonder what enemies did he make that would want him dead.

Shortly after Pearson had ended his call, Monique strolled into the room. She looked a lot more subdued than she did when she left to work. Pearson could tell that his little fixer liked to sweep things under the rug when it came to her own problems. Monique had buried herself in work instead of talking to him about what happened at lunch with her ex.

"You look tense. Everything okay?" Monique asked as she cocked her head to the side.

"I'm fine. Long day," Pearson stated with a heavy sigh.

He wasn't going to bombard her with all of his bullshit. Yes, she was the "fixer" but she definitely didn't sign up to play murder she wrote. Monique fixed reputations, she wasn't *Nancy Drew*.

"Pearson, sweetie, I know that my personal life invaded our good time, and I'm really sorry about that. I promise that it won't happen again. Even if I have to call Damon, so that we can meet up and hash this all out. It won't interfere with my job."

Pearson wanted to smile at the fact that she'd thought his mood was because of what had happened earlier, but he couldn't focus on that because he could've sworn that she said she would call that douche of an ex. However, he had to be hearing things. There wasn't any way while the world was still turning, and he was still breathing that he would let Monique face that bastard for his sake.

"There's no reason for you to meet up with your ex. He's an asshole. It's done between you two, right?" Pearson could feel himself getting angry at the thought of Monique still wanting her ex, especially with what Pearson knew about the bastard.

"Of course, it's over. I just don't want him popping up and causing problems for the remainder of the conference. That's all." Monique frowned.

"Good. Because it would kill me if my wife was in love with another man."

Monique sighed. "Pearson, it was cute at first, you calling me wife. But it's weird that you insist on calling me that. Why would someone who only had relationships of convenience suddenly get a kick out of calling me wife? I don't get it."

Pearson shook his head. "Because you *are* my wife, Monique. We got married last night. For real."

Monique chuckled, and when she took in his face, he could see that she realized he wasn't joking.

"Wait. What do you mean *for real*?"

"Monique, we signed a marriage license last night. We had witnesses and we stood in front of an ordained minister..."

"But it was *Elvis!*" she yelled throwing up her hands in frustration.

"And this is Vegas." Pearson shrugged.

"I... I... What the hell did I do?" Monique whispered.

"You married, me baby, till death do us part." Pearson smiled wide. *I told Dom I would handle it. She will be just fine.*

Before he could finish the thought, Monique fainted.

19

FALLING

Monique woke up with a slight headache and a frown. She looked up at a ceiling that was unfamiliar. *Where am I? And what was I doing?* She thought as she sat up slowly trying to get her wits about her.

"Holy shit!" It all came rushing back.

"You faint, and wake up cursing? That can't be good." Pearson sat in a chair facing the king-sized bed. He looked completely stressed out. His hair was in complete disarray and his face was filled with worry.

"Are you okay?" Monique asked, concerned. Even with everything she'd seen Pearson go through, this was the worse she had ever seen him look.

He chuckled as he came to sit next to her. "You've been out for hours and you ask if *I'm* okay. You're one in a million."

Monique smiled up at him, but she was still worried about his haggard appearance.

"Wait. Did you say I fainted? I don't remember fainting." Monique frowned again.

"Do you remember anything? The doctor coming in and checking on you? Nothing?" Pearson asked frowning in return.

"I remember you saying that we were actually married, which can't be right, right?" Monique asked.

Pearson sighed heavily. "If you keep asking me that, you're going to give me a complex."

"Pearson, I thought we were just having a laugh. There is no way we could actually be married. There's paperwork that has to be filed." She shook her head in disbelief.

"Monique," Pearson sighed when he said her name. "For the last time, we're in Vegas. All that stuff we talked about with *Elvis* was us agreeing to be married. We signed our names, and the chapel files it with the state. I specifically asked you if you were sure."

"I wasn't paying attention to that. I thought it was all a campy setup for tourists. I thought it took more than that to really get married." Monique felt so silly. How could she not know that she was really marrying Pearson? *Girl, you need to get out more if that's all it takes.*

"Well, it's done now. We are husband and wife." Pearson's face turned smug, and Monique had to wonder if he was actually crazy.

"Pearson, we have to get this annulled," Monique stated exasperated.

"We can't do that. It will ruin our reputations." His face was still smug and Monique wanted to slap the smirk off his handsome face.

Monique had been in many situations. She ran scenarios for a living, but being married to Pearson Grant after knowing him for a little over two months and having some quickie wedding in Vegas of all things, was one scenario that had never crossed her mind.

How the hell had she been so dumb? Monique could spend all the time in the world beating herself up about it, but that wouldn't help her fix it. She needed a solution to this situation for her and her client.

"You're right. If it gets out that we got married in Vegas and then got it annulled, there will be too many questions. People will think that I'm incompetent and make rash decisions, and my business can't take that. Hell, yours can't either," Monique stated, thinking out loud.

She had to talk her way through the problem. It was her way of dealing with the situation. Pearson seemed to understand what she was doing and simply nodded without interrupting her. Monique smiled internally at his thoughtfulness.

Sometimes, it was like they were so in sync that she wondered how they were ever at odds with each other at the beginning. He seemed to understand her better than she could ever expect. That both scared and overwhelmed her. *This man is my husband. I guess I could do worse.*

"We don't have to get it annulled right now, but we will keep this quiet," Monique stated out loud, again she was really just talking to herself. "People will think it's some sort of stunt, and we don't want that. If someone finds out and asks, we will just say that we wanted to enjoy our newlywed status in private. That should keep the vultures at bay."

"So, I finally have a wife, and I can't even introduce you as such?" Pearson looked more than a little annoyed and Monique wondered what his deal was.

"I don't think it's a good idea. We need to keep this on the low. It's one thing being your fake girlfriend, it is a completely different story being your real wife."

"You're right. It is a completely different story. I didn't go into this blind, Monique. I knew what we were doing." Pearson responded.

Monique wanted to be pissed that he knew that she thought it was a joke, and he knew it was real the whole time, but she couldn't be mad at him for her foolish actions. *And I can't even blame it on being drunk,* Monique thought as she shook her head in disappointment.

Monique sighed as she flopped back on the bed, "We went from zero to a million so quick with this. I just don't know how to fix it. I'm sorry."

Monique was always so careful, and not even a full twenty-four hours in Vegas and she had lost her damn mind. She had no idea what to do next. And for the first time, nothing came to mind. She was officially stuck.

But at least Pearson's problems were dwindling. Darlene hadn't been in the news anymore since Pearson's interview ratings beat hers, and he hadn't been a trending topic since the accident. So maybe, this wouldn't be a big thing, and they could quietly get it annulled in a few weeks when Pearson was off of everyone's radar.

Okay, so keep it quiet. Then take care of it in due time. Nobody has to know I not only slept with my client while still working for him, but married him too. What the hell kind of fixer am I? Sweet baby Jesus, what have I done?

"You don't have to be sorry, and there's nothing for you to fix." Pearson's deep voice penetrated her detrimental thoughts.

"Everything will be just fine. We were having fun. We are in Vegas." Pearson continued.

"Don't remind me," Monique interrupted with a grumble.

Pearson chuckled and pulled Monique into his arms. She didn't protest or fight. She just went willingly. She could admit that his arms were a comfort to her, and she desperately needed comfort.

"Just trust me. Have I steered you wrong?" Pearson asked, his eyes gleaming.

"I haven't really let you steer, but we got married while I was driving, so..."

Pearson laughed lightly, and the sound made Monique smile. "I would ride with you anywhere, my beautiful wife."

Monique shook her head although she continued to smile. "Remember we keep this between us, so calling me wife is not a good idea."

"Between us. Right. I can do that." Monique saw Pearson's smile falter just slightly and she frowned.

Monique had a feeling that Pearson was not happy about their secret marriage, but she had to protect herself. *What if this doesn't work, and it all falls apart? I have to keep from falling, no matter what!*

MONIQUE COULD HEAR herself moaning in her sleep, but she couldn't stop the wonderful feeling of pleasure that was heating her entire body, starting with her core. Her body had a mind of its own, her hips were moving from side to side in a swaying motion, her legs were lifting her lower body in an up and down motion. *Damn that feels good; too good to be a dream.*

Monique cracked open her sleepy eyes, and found the source of her pleasure. Pearson was between her thighs, feasting on her creamy center like she was the breakfast buffet. He was licking and tasting the lips of her pussy like a mad man, and the feeling was glorious.

She moaned again, but not just from the feeling, from the sight of his head between her thighs moving from side to side. When she gripped his hair tightly in ecstasy, his lust-filled eyes locked in on her. They twinkled with passion, and she could cum from the look alone. However, his tongue was what actually did the job.

"Pearson! I'm cumming! Don't stop! Ummmm..." Monique groaned lustfully as her entire body exploded from his actions.

Before her orgasm finished, Pearson climbed up her body and pushed his massive cock into her still quivering pussy. They groaned in unison at the feeling.

The connection they had was like no other, and Monique couldn't deny it. She had been trying to deny it, but that was no longer an option. It wasn't just the sex. At least, to her it wasn't and that could be a problem. However, right now, sex is what was being offered; so that's what she would take.

"You feel so fucking good, wife. You have the best pussy, baby. I could eat you all day, but there's nothing like fucking you." Pearson's dirty words only served to make her wetter. Monique could only moan in agreement.

Their bodies moved in synchronicity, they became one in their desires. The erotic sounds of their moans chorused throughout the room. The sweet melody of their combined lust ramping up their body temperatures to an overheated frenzied explosion.

"You feel so good. Fuck me harder!" Monique demanded.

The way Pearson handled her body made her feel free, wanton, and absolutely desirable. He caressed and cherished her, but he also fucked her like a man out of control. She needed the latter.

Pearson began to pump into her wildly. Monique could feel him hardening even more as he ground into her g-spot. Her legs began to tremble, her toes curled, and her nails scraped down his back as she screamed out her release.

"Yes, beautiful! Give it all to me! Damn this pussy is wet." Pearson pumped his hips passionately bringing Monique to the brink once again.

"You're going to make me cum again. Fuck! Shit!" Monique's words were incoherent, yelling out her bliss as she came again.

"Damn!" Pearson exploded deep inside her core.

After their breathing subsided, Pearson got up and went to the bathroom, he came back with a warm washcloth and cleaned her up. That's when Monique realized they had once again failed to use protection. *What the hell is wrong with me?*

Monique looked suspiciously at Pearson. It was like he hypnotized her whenever they had sex. She would go into a trance behind his miraculous dick, and she made stupid decisions. *I never had these issues in the past. I also never had dick this good either,* Monique thought as she watched her new husband lay down on the bed with a smile brightening his entire face. Monique decided not to worry about condoms because she was on the shot and technically, he was her husband so at least one of her rules was still intact.

"You're pretty proud of yourself, aren't you?" Monique smiled lazily.

Pearson turned to face her. "I just had my favorite breakfast of all time, and my wife has a look of satisfaction written all over her lovely face. Why wouldn't I be happy?"

Monique blushed. She liked when he talked dirty, but it still wasn't something she was used to yet.

"You sure know how to flatter a girl." Monique reached up and ran her hand over his unshaven jaw. It was different waking up with him today. It felt somehow more real, and she couldn't put her finger on why.

Pearson leaned over and kissed her lips softly. "If you haven't noticed, I will do anything to see you smile. It is one of my most favorite things in the world."

Monique cocked her head to the side and took a good look at the man that she barely knew, but somehow ended up married to. The sincerity was written all over his face. There wasn't any arrogance, smugness, or underlying meanings to his words. He was being real with her, and it meant more to her than she cared to admit.

"You surprise me sometimes," Monique confessed. "I don't know what to expect from this man in front of me." She kissed his lips softly.

"You can expect all of me. And I expect all of you." Pearson didn't smile or blink as he held her gaze, and she knew that he meant every word. But Monique didn't know if she could give him all of her. This was just a temporary situation, so what would she do after they were done?

However, there was nothing that her brain could tell her heart that would keep her from falling for this man.

20

COMING TO LIGHT

Pearson couldn't believe his luck. Having Monique as his wife wasn't something that he ever thought possible. Hell, he didn't even have the thought. Marriage hadn't been on his radar. Pearson thought he would be a perpetual bachelor. He would have his companions until his death. Now that he was married, he couldn't think of anyone else that he would rather have as his bride.

He knew that she thought that they would keep it a secret, and then dissolve their marriage without a second thought. She was very much mistaken. Pearson may not have planned to get married, but now that he was, divorce or annulment was not an option.

Pearson had to make Monique believe that they could be happy together. He had to keep reminding her of the chemistry they shared. He reluctantly gave her some space, and left her to do her own thing while he attended the summit. Pearson didn't realize how much he would miss her in just a few hours, he also didn't realize that he could be such a sap.

Pearson sighed as he entered the suite; he had had a long day of boring conference meetings and presentations. *Now I remember why I always skipped these types of events.*

However, Monique was right yet again, and he was able to make a few more connections that would be helpful for the launch of his new division. Mark would be ecstatic that the release of the division would be back on track. With all the foolishness that had been happening, they decided it would be good for the company to push back the announcement. Nobody wanted the new division's opening to be overshadowed by the chaos that was happening with Pearson.

However, if things kept going according to Monique's plan, then Pearson would be out of the headlines and his company could move in a positive direction.

Pearson's phone rang as he entered the suite. He looked around for Monique, but he didn't see her. "She must've gone out," Pearson said into the empty room.

"Hello?" He answered his phone.

"Hey, Pearson. How's everything going? You know, since you left me to look after the company and went to God knows where without even so much as a see ya later," Mark stated with annoyance lacing his every word.

Pearson didn't let the man get under his skin. He knew that his VP was temperamental and nervous about everything. So his anxiousness didn't bother Pearson in the slightest. *Not like it used to.*

"Mark, everything is going great actually. I decided to come to the Global Stage Tech Summit. I've made quite a few connections that could potentially get our new division back on track."

"You're in Vegas?" Pearson could hear the surprise in his VP's voice, and he understood it. Because Pearson was not one to voluntarily go to any type of conference.

"Yes. The summit is a good place to network and get some business deals done, and I can stay out of the spotlight." Pearson replied.

"Right. You definitely need to stay out of the spotlight." Mark sighed before he continued. "Does Keifer know where you are? Because I'm pretty sure he's been calling the office looking for you."

"No. Nobody knows where I am. I'm staying out of the press, remember? Don't worry, though. I'll get in touch with Keifer," Pearson replied.

"Alright. Well things are going just fine around here. Just so you know," Mark stated his voice held a note of irritation, and Pearson wondered not for the first time, why the man was so uneasy.

"I know that my company is in good hands, Mark. I trust you," Pearson replied.

"I would say stay out of trouble, but..." Mark trailed off, and Pearson wanted to resent the man's words, but how could he? The last few months of his life had been nothing but trouble.

Pearson and Mark spoke for a few moments longer and then disconnected the call. Pearson felt better with Mark being in the office. Media Tech Innovation was his baby, and he wanted it to thrive no matter what anyone else thought.

When he figured out why someone was trying to kill him, Pearson decided that he would take a much needed vacation. *Maybe I can talk the wife into a lavish honeymoon.* Pearson smiled at the thought. Monique Carter was now Mrs. Pearson Grant. *Who'd a thought?*

"Pearson? Are you here?" Monique called from the living room of the suite. Pearson sauntered out of the bedroom before she could make her way to him.

As soon as Pearson saw her, his yearning for her couldn't be controlled. He pushed her up against the nearest wall pinning her in place with his strong muscular frame. Pearson's tongue pummeled her mouth. Monique gasped in surprise when he lifted her off of her feet.

She instinctively wrapped her legs around his waist, the casual dress that she wore sliding up her thighs. Her hands went to his hair with a tug, and he growled low into her mouth. He really liked that she played a little rough at times. He also figured out that she liked when he talked dirty.

"I missed you today." Monique groaned as Pearson kissed and nipped at the sensitive skin on her neck.

"Did you now?" Pearson continued to nibble at her throat. Her taste drove him to the brink of madness. He would never get used to the way she made him feel.

"I did. I was bored without you here holding me captive in your bed." She giggled when he pulled her earlobe into his mouth playfully.

"I think you are the one holding me captive. I mean what man in his right mind could walk away from a goddess like you? Not a sane one, I guarantee you that." Pearson continued to kiss all along her neck and chest until she started to grind against his hardening member.

"Wife... You know I won't be able to stop if you keep doing that?" Pearson didn't know if he was begging for her to keep going or to stop.

"But it feels so good. I don't think I can stop." Monique continued to roll her hips seductively, and Pearson lost it.

He was pretty sure that his new wife liked making him lose control. Actually, he knew for a fact that she liked him losing control.

Pearson lowered them both to the floor, he easily slipped the loose dress over her head, and was mesmerized by her glowing ebony skin. He hooked his fingers into her small panties and slipped them down her legs.

"Now, it's time for a little afternoon delight." Pearson smiled devilishly as he made his way to his little piece of heaven on earth.

AFTER THEIR TRYST, Pearson and Monique took a much needed nap. However, what she'd said earlier about being held captive made him make plans for a special night out.

Pearson never thought he would ever be in a situation like this, but now that he was, he wanted to make sure that Monique knew that she was special to him. Pearson left her sleeping in the massive bed as he made arrangements for their date.

It was nice to have a semblance of a somewhat normal life again. He was just another face in the crowd in Vegas. He wasn't a trending topic or a tech millionaire. He was just a guy on vacation.

Pearson was just finishing his call as he gazed out the massive windows at the view of the Vegas strip. Although the streets were packed with people and the lights glittered and danced brightening up the night sky, it still gave him a sense of calmness that he hadn't felt before.

Pearson was in deep concentration when he felt a pair of small hands caress his back and move around to his chest. Monique's delicate hands fluttered through the light hairs on his torso.

"I woke up and you were gone. I thought I dreamt this whole thing 'cause no dick could be that good." Monique laughed as Pearson swung her around in front of him playfully.

"You can have as much of this good dick as you can take, my wife. Now, let's get dressed so we can go out. I have plans for us." Pearson replied with a smile and a wink.

This is going to be fun.

IT WASN'T FUN. In fact, it was the biggest cluster fuck that Pearson had experienced since the Darlene debacle. *I can't believe this is my life right now!*

The night started off with a promise. Pearson had reserved a table at *Tao*, because Monique had mentioned that she'd seen it online and would like to eat there. When they arrived, the place was absolutely packed; their reservations had been set for the wrong time, and they would've had to wait two extra hours. It wouldn't have been a problem except it was a Saturday night and every place they decided to go was also booked.

No problem. They were in Vegas. There were restaurants everywhere. However, out of all the restaurants on the strip, they walked into the one where none other than Damon Hicks, Monique's ex was dining. Still not that bad, except... he wasn't alone. Pearson immediately recognized the woman from the pictures that Dom showed him a month earlier. Pearson never brought up what he knew because Monique had already broken up with Damon, but that may have been a mistake. However, Pearson decided that would be one secret he took to the grave.

"The fuck is happening right now?" Pearson saw when Monique had spotted the two on the patio of the establishment, and before Pearson could blink, she was confronting them.

"Moni, what... what are you doing here?" the woman stammered, wide-eyed.

"What am *I* doing here? What the hell are you doing here with *him*?" Monique questioned with fury written all over her face.

Pearson wanted to intervene and keep Monique from getting hurt, but it was good that she'd found out about the two of them now. Everyone needed closure and from the looks of things, this was definitely the end for Mr. Hicks and his date.

"Damon must've forgotten to mention that I saw him the other day." Both women glared at Damon, and Pearson knew the other man was up shit creek without a paddle.

"No, he didn't mention it. But we've been busy. Besides, what are you so mad about? Ya'll aren't together anymore," Nikki said dismissively, and Pearson was surprised that Monique didn't fly across the table and punch her because that's what he would've done.

Pearson could see the fire burning in Monique's eyes. The betrayal she must've felt and the lies she had to have endured for who knows how long. It was a travesty.

"I can't believe you would do this to me, Nikki. You were my friend. I trusted you." Pearson could hear the hurt in Monique's voice, but there weren't any tears as she shot daggers at the woman who'd claimed to be her friend.

"I told your ass time and time again to stop wasting time with a man that you didn't want." Nikki shrugged. "It's not my fault he chose me."

"Any man would choose free pussy. You ought to know, since you're forever giving it out," Monique stated matter-of-factly. "But my problem isn't with you. Although you're a lying good for nothing bitch, I have to say thanks for taking that asshole off my hands. My problem is with you." Monique looked toward Damon, and he stood up. Pearson had been standing quietly by observing, but it was time for him to step in. The last thing that Damon would be able to do is step to Monique aggressively while he was around. *I will beat the holy fuck out of him.*

Pearson pulled a seething Monique to his side, and she slid beneath his arm without protest. He wrapped his arm around her and kissed the top of her head lovingly. Pearson could feel the tension leave her body, and he was glad to be able to lend her the comfort that she seemed to need.

"I think you need to sit your ass back down before you do something that will get you hurt." Pearson's face was filled with menace, and if Damon so much as breathed wrong, he would fuck him up.

"You stay the fuck out of this. Why are you even fucking here? This has nothing to do with you. Monique *works* for you. Do you go around defending all of the help?" Damon questioned smugly with a smirk.

"*The help*?" Pearson laughed darkly. *I'm going to break his mother-fucking neck.* "I know you didn't just call my wife the fucking help?" Pearson's words were loud and began to draw attention, but the fury he felt couldn't be controlled, and before he knew it, his fists were already balled.

21

EYE OF THE STORM

I t all happened so fast. One moment Monique was arguing with her ex and her skank of an ex-friend, and the next moment, she was trying to keep Pearson from going to jail. Monique saw when his emotions turned stormy, and his body tensed. But when that creepy-ass laugh left his mouth, Monique knew that all hell was about to break loose.

On a normal day, Monique would never get between two grown men fighting. However, today, she would not let her new husband get into an all-out brawl because of her. She should've never engaged with Damon's trifling ass or Nikki's. They weren't worth a damn and they wouldn't get to ruin anything for Monique.

However, before she could make a move, Damon swung at Pearson and clipped his jaw. The punch didn't stun Pearson at all because before she knew it, he was slugging the shit out of Damon right where he stood.

Monique's mouth was hanging open because she couldn't believe that the men were fighting. Before the fight could get out of hand, security ran in and broke them up. Because the fight was broken up so fast, and they were ushered out the back door in a flash, Monique was pretty certain that nobody even noticed the commotion.

I guess security in Vegas is used to this sort of thing.

The four of them stood in the back of the building with security hovering between them, and Monique knew that she had to calm Pearson down and get him out of there before anybody recognized who he was.

Damon was still shooting daggers in their direction as he spit blood on the ground from his busted lip, and Nikki stood beside him with an evil smirk on her lips. Monique couldn't believe she'd ever called the woman a friend.

"Pearson, please let's go before this gets any worse. I don't think anybody noticed you fighting, but we can't take the chance." Monique tried her best to reason with the furious looking gorgeous man in front of her.

"He called you the help. The fucking help, Monique." Pearson's voice was a low steady growl. Monique had never really seen him this mad before. He'd been upset and even angry, but right now the man before her was absolutely livid.

"Aren't you the one who says you shouldn't give a fuck what people have to say." Monique's eyebrow raised in challenge. Pearson usually couldn't stand to pass up a challenge, and Monique was hoping that was the case today.

"This is different," Pearson responded stubbornly, shaking his head. His hair falling over his eyes with the movement. *Damn he's sexy when he's mad. Shit, focus Moni.*

"No, baby it isn't," Monique said sweetly, caressing his jaw softly. She kissed the corner of his mouth trying her hardest to get Pearson to look at her. He was breathing hard and staring in Damon's direction but the security guards were standing firmly between them.

Monique wondered if they knew who Pearson was or if they did this for just any old guy off the street. When Pearson took a step forward as if he was going to go after Damon again, Monique knew that reasoning with him wouldn't work. She had to calm him down another way.

Monique decided she would use every weapon in her arsenal to get him to calm down. Kissing, sweetness, hell she would hump his damn leg if it would get him to leave without knocking Damon out. It was about more than their reputations, or even their businesses. This was about seeing the man that she was falling for protecting her. Pearson was a different person now than when she first met him, he was kind and considerate and Monique just couldn't allow all the progress they made to go down the drain.

When she ran her finger over his pink bottom lip, Pearson looked at her finally. His eyes still glowed with anger, but at least his breathing had slowed and his red face had returned back to its normal color.

"I can't let him talk to you like that. I have to beat his ass. It's the principle," Pearson responded, looking at her with pleading eyes.

It was simply ridiculous that a grown man was giving her the "puppy dog" look, so that he could beat up another grown man. Monique knew that Pearson was sincere in his protectiveness, so she wouldn't roll her eyes at the complete foolishness of the situation.

Monique kissed his lips again, and Pearson relaxed slightly. However, she knew that if she didn't get him to leave now it was no telling what he might do. "Fuck him."

Pearson shook his head, but a smirk covered his once scowling lips. They gazed at each other having a silent conversation. It was like they were in their own world once again. Everything around them seemed to stop, and nothing else mattered. When the storm cleared from his eyes, Monique knew that everything would be okay.

However, Monique could hear Damon and Nikki still talking shit behind them. There was nothing she wanted more than to kick their asses. But the punch that Pearson had gotten in, and Damon's bloodied lip and wounded pride would have to do. Although Monique wanted to get her hands on that backstabbing heffa, Nikki, she would let it go. The woman did her a favor in the end, she was rid of a cheating boyfriend, and a jealous fake friend.

However, Monique still couldn't believe that she never put two and two together. The way they shared secret little looks and smiles when they were around one another. Monique shook her head, *fuck both of them! They don't get to make a fool of me anymore.*

"Let's get out of here. You can take me to eat, so that I can have you for dessert," Monique purred at Pearson.

"What the hell did you just say?" Damon asked behind her, but Monique refused to turn around and break her focus on Pearson.

"I told you she was fucking him. She probably has been all along. But you want to feel guilty. Pshh," Nikki replied hatefully.

Monique didn't turn around to see the trifling whore's face, but she knew that Nikki was smiling. Monique could hear the glee in her voice as she accused her of being a cheater.

How could I have been so blind? She was as jealous as they came. Always taking shots and throwing shade, and she always had something to say about my relationship. And here I was thinking it was my sister that was sleeping with Damon. Monique shook her head at herself for being so stubborn.

"I thought he was a *client*. I thought the almighty Monique would never fuck a client," Nikki taunted. Normally, Nikki's accusations would've hurt Monique. Always wanting to be perfect and fix everything, she would've gone into a tailspin of depression and guilt.

But today was a new day. And she was a new Monique.

"Of course, I'm fucking him, bitch. He's my husband," Monique threw over her shoulder as she grabbed Pearson's hand and sauntered away. *Welp, so much for keeping our marriage a secret.*

THE NEXT MORNING, Monique lay wrapped in Pearson's strong arms, her fingers lazily running through the fine hairs on his chest. It was amazing how much comfort she got from just being in his arms. She never would've predicted that this would be her life.

Pearson kissed the top of her head and nuzzled her hair, bringing Monique out of her thoughts. She looked up at him smiling with contentment. After their argument with Damon and Nikki, they came back to their suite and ordered room service. Monique didn't want to have to deal with the bustle of crowds and busy restaurants. She just wanted to go back into their magical fun bubble that they were immersed in before her ex came and busted it.

The things that both Damon and Nikki said showed Monique just how well they both knew her. They played on her biggest fears and insecurities. And although she held steadfast in front of them, and she told herself in the moment that she wouldn't let them get to her. In reality, their words had hurt her deeply.

Monique worked hard not to be just another piece of ass, getting clients based on her looks. She left Bedford and Stein because she felt like the token they paraded around to get minority clients, most of whom were men. She wanted to earn her clientele based on merit. Her intelligence, and willingness to do her job no matter what; that was what got her clients.

Word of mouth from doing a spectacular job got Monique her first clients, and she had been steady when it came to building her business.

Now, she lay in bed the morning after the disastrous evening, her mind racing a mile a minute. *Was this a mistake? Will I lose credibility? Will I lose all that I've worked for? Shit!*

"Hey, gorgeous. What's going on in that gorgeous head of yours?" Pearson's voice was a deep rumble. His questioning gazed locked in on hers when she looked up at him.

"Nothing," Monique mumbled not wanting to voice her concerns worried it would bring them to fruition.

"You know, wife, I've wanted to spank that juicy ass of yours. So you lying to my face is a good enough reason to bend you over my knee."

His words were playful, but Monique was beginning to recognize when Pearson was serious. She arched an eyebrow at him, for the first time ever, Monique knew that she was down for a little spanking.

"What's on your mind, beautiful?" Pearson asked again.

"I've never been so reckless and I'm feeling guilty." Monique sighed heavily before continuing. "I just don't want hasty decisions to ruin what either of us have worked so hard for."

"Baby, stop worrying about things you have no control over. If my business can survive me all these years, both of our companies will be just fine." Pearson tried to reassure her, but Monique wasn't totally convinced.

Monique wanted to believe there wouldn't be any blow back from their lack of judgement, but she just couldn't shake the foreboding feeling in her gut.

"Beautiful, it will be..."

Pearson didn't get to finish his sentence because both of their phones went off. Pearson reached for his and began to scroll, but Monique didn't want to look. She didn't want to face the fact that she had royally fucked up. This time she couldn't just sweep the mess that *she* made under the rug. Monique had to deal with it, her personal and professional life depended on it.

Pearson was eerily still and quiet, and it just made Monique that much more apprehensive. However, she took a deep breath, and grabbed her phone. There were so many notifications, she didn't know what to look at first.

"Shit! This is bad," she said out loud, but Pearson's face was still blank, showing no emotions, and Monique knew that his blank face was almost as bad as a furious one.

The headlines were endless and there were pictures to go along with each one. She and Pearson were laughing and dancing. There was even a picture of the argument with Damon. But at least there wasn't video of the punch. Monique sighed in relief. Whoever seemed to be stalking them didn't get the fight on camera. But what was on film was them kissing in front of Elvis the minister.

"Well, looks like the cat's out of the bag." Pearson's blank face gave way to a bright smile. And it was genuine smile. Not a famous Pearson smirk or even his wolf-like grin he sometimes displayed. Monique stared at him in confusion.

Why in the hell is he smiling?

"You seem happy about this." Monique watched him closely. As close as they had grown over the past few months, she still didn't know him very well.

"Why wouldn't I be happy? I'm married to a beautiful, intelligent, strong, and loving woman. And *everyone* knows she's mine," Pearson responded his smile growing wider.

Monique was flattered by his words, and she even felt her face heat. But that didn't negate the fact that she thought he was crazy as hell.

"I know how I want to handle this, but it's not just about me. I can tell you my plan, and then we can strategize. How's that sound?" Monique questioned.

"That sounds great, but after we have shower sex." Pearson's smile was the predatory one that Monique was used to, and she laughed and kissed his lips.

He pulled her toward the lavish ensuite bathroom, and turned on the water. The shower was all glass and could probably fit about ten people. It had multiple shower heads pointing in all different directions. The hot water relaxed her tension-filled body. Monique wished she could just live in this fairytale forever. She hated that the one time that she let herself relax she dragged someone's image into her mess.

"Hey." Pearson kissed the back of her neck as his strong arms wrapped around her waist from behind. "Stop."

Monique sighed. She wished that it was that easy for her. But she knew that she would be wound up until she found a solution to help the situation.

"I'm sorry. I just hate feeling like I this. Especially because of something I did." Monique turned in Pearson's strong arms, and leaned her head on his bare naked chest.

"Something we did. I thought you wanted to talk *after* we had shower sex?" Pearson stuck his lip out in an adorable pout that was so unlike him that Monique giggled.

"Okay. So if it's after the shower sex, I guess you better get to sexing me up then." Monique smiled as Pearson dropped to his knees.

Well, I'll be damned.

22

WHEN IT RAINS IT POURS

Pearson dropped to his knees to pleasure his wife. *His wife.* He still couldn't believe she was his. He never would've imagined that a woman like Monique would ever be his. Pearson could admit that he was a tad bit obsessed, but it was more than that now. He was glad that she had come into his life, and she would continue to be there... *Forever.* He thought with a smile as he licked his lips.

He knew she would do her best to try to keep their marriage a secret, and now that it was in the media, she couldn't. Pearson didn't know how it got out that they were even in Vegas, but he wasn't particularly sad about the news of their marriage being reported in the media.

Pearson shook his head to clear his thoughts. The last thing he wanted to be thinking about while defiling his wife in the shower was the media. Pearson regained his focus which wasn't a hard thing to do with Monique's gloriously naked flesh in his face. Her curvaceous body was slick and glistening with water. Her perky breasts sat high and her black cherry-colored nipples were hard and waiting for Pearson to suckle. But his attention was further down her luxurious body.

Pearson pushed his wet hair out of his face; the dripping water was ruining his view and he couldn't have that. He leaned in and licked Monique's juicy center. Her taste was scrumptious and exotic and he couldn't get enough. She thrusts her hips seductively moaning loudly. The sound bounced off the gigantic shower walls heightening Pearson's lust. He grabbed her ass cheeks and aggressively squeezed them. He had never been so thankful to have large hands in his life. Her round plump bottom was the greatest gift a man could have the pleasure of viewing.

"Spread your legs wider," Pearson demanded as he continued to lavish in the taste of her core.

Monique's moans became outright screams when Pearson pulled her sensitive clit into his mouth and sucked hard. When he added a finger, she began to buck and ride his hand and face.

"That's it, gorgeous. Ride my fucking face. I love that shit. You taste so fucking delicious," Pearson egged her on with his words. Her thrusts became erratic when he added another finger.

"Don't stop. I'm gonna cum. Oh shit! Hell yeah!" Monique's hips were wild as her climax hit her. Pearson could feel the gush of wetness flow from her body into his mouth and he lapped at her pussy like a man dying of thirst.

Pearson slurped and licked until Monique's body finally calmed. He then raised up off his knees and kissed her passionately. He easily slipped his hardened cock within her wet slippery center. Pearson relished in the tight hold that her pussy had on his manhood. He moaned at the sweet torturous feeling.

He threw his head back and picked Monique up while still nestled inside of her. She wrapped her thick thighs around his flanks and began to propel herself up and down his cock. His dick was slippery from her arousal and the water. The feeling was heaven, and he could feel his orgasm building, but he wasn't ready to cum so he held Monique still.

"Nooooo." Monique whined trying to move her hips. "Baby please let me cum."

"Be still." Pearson commanded kissing her roughly. He pushed her against the wall of the shower to keep her steady. He took a deep breath when he felt her tighten her inner muscles around his shaft.

"Fuck. Monique, dammit. Stop!" Pearson was damn near pleading with her, but she just smirked, and did it again.

"No. Make me cum," she sang as she kept up the movement.

Pearson could no longer resist the sweet sensation. He began pounding into her roughly. He knew that he would lose control, but she had pushed him over the edge. He could no longer keep the wild thrusting of his hips in check.

"Yes, fuck me!" Monique screamed as Pearson continued to pound her pussy. When she finally let out a scream full of ecstasy, Pearson let himself go.

He pushed his cock deep into her weeping pussy. Their moans of desire rang out in unison as they simultaneously reached their climax. Their breaths came out rough and ragged for what seemed like forever.

"Shit, that was good." Pearson said as he nuzzled the side of Monique's neck.

"It sure the hell was." Monique agreed with a sigh.

"Let's get dried off, so we can get something to eat. I've worked up an appetite." Pearson smacked a kiss on Monique's lips as he finally removed himself from her with a wince. He placed her on her feet and she stood on shaky legs.

"I know my hair looks a hot damn mess." Monique ran her hand through her loosened bun. She untangled the band that was holding her hair up and wrung the water out.

Pearson smiled as he watched her. He never thought that he'd be watching a woman wash her hair, and actually enjoying it. *I'm officially obsessed.*

"You look beautiful," Pearson said honestly. He knew without any doubt in his mind that Monique was the most beautiful woman he had ever had the pleasure of seeing.

He used to think that having big boobs, long legs, and a nice ass was all it took to be beautiful. But now, he knew the truth. Those superficial things were nice to look at, but they didn't equal beauty. Not real beauty anyway.

Real beauty is what was standing in front of him. A woman that was compassionate, loving, giving and kind. Who would go out of her way to help other people without reward or recognition. A woman whose internal beauty rivaled that of a saint, at least to Pearson.

Monique wasn't just beautiful, she was simply unforgettable, and Pearson would spend the rest of his days telling her just how much he loved her.

Yep, it's official. I'm in love with this woman.

"So your big plan is to say nothing?" Pearson asked Monique, confusion coloring his handsome face. He couldn't believe after everything that she still wanted to hide their relationship.

"Listen, we need to just get through this conference and we will make a joint statement when we get back to Dallas," Monique answered with an exasperated sigh.

"I thought you said hiding from the press only makes them chase you harder." Pearson's face was smug because he knew that she wasn't thinking with her professional hat, she was thinking as a woman in a relationship.

After a minute of silent staring with narrowed eyes, Monique sighed again.

"Fine. You're right. We will release a statement now, saying that we are indeed married, and we would like privacy at this time." Monique flopped down on the couch. She had been pacing back in forth in front of the massive windows since they'd started the conversation.

Pearson knew that it was something that she did while she was thinking, so he just sat by patiently, and watched her work. And Lord did he like to watch her work. *Damn, my wife is fucking hot!*

"Who do you think leaked it?" Monique asked. "Never mind, I

know it was probably that bitch Nikki, or that even bigger *bitch,* Damon."

Pearson nodded. He thought the same thing. Plus, the only other people who knew they were married was Dom and Venus. Dom wouldn't say a word, and Venus thought it was a joke, because Monique had never called her back to clarify that it was real.

"I'm sorry. I should've thought about what I was saying, but that hoe just made me so mad. Accusing me of sleeping with you while I was in a relationship. I would never."

"Babe, we both know nothing happened until I seduced you when we got to Vegas. It's not your fault that you couldn't resist all of my charms." Pearson raised his eyebrows up and down suggestively. Monique rolled her eyes, but she chuckled at his antics. He loved to hear her laugh even if it was just a small one.

"You're so silly." Monique slapped at him playfully. "But really, before we make any announcements, I have to call my mother."

"Okay, I'm sure it will be fine. I mean you're a grown woman, right?"

By the look on Monique's pretty heart-shaped face, he was almost sure that calling her mother wasn't going to be a smooth as it should be.

"I am a grown woman, but please believe, your new mother-in-law will never forgive you for marrying me in Vegas."

Pearson stood and walked over to Monique making her stop her pacing. He bent his head and kissed her lips softly. He slowly took both of her arms and wrapped them around his neck. Monique gave him a shy smile as he placed his forehead against hers.

Pearson wrapped his arms around her waist and smiled down at her. "I will give you whatever kind of wedding you want, wherever you want it. You can tell your mother that we just couldn't wait another day without being married. I'm sure she will understand. And if she doesn't..." Pearson shrugged his massive shoulders before he continued, "then just blame it on me."

"Oh, you have no idea who Mrs. Luanne Carter is. She will tear you to shreds and pray for you all in the same breath. You don't want to be on her bad side, believe me." Monique shook her head looking worried.

Pearson hated that she was upset about telling her mother about their nuptials. He didn't think about telling his family. All he had left was his aunt and uncle and his cousin, Kelsey. His parents had passed years before, and he didn't have any siblings.

"I'm sorry that I didn't even think about your family." Pearson rubbed the back of his neck. He wasn't used to feeling so much.

Pearson did what he wanted when he wanted. He didn't have to answer to other people, and he sure as hell didn't think about how other people felt. It was all new to him.

"It's okay. We will deal with it. Just promise if you can't handle this, let's just end it now without making any type of announcement. Reputations be damned. We have to be all in or all out." Monique was looking deeply into his eyes, and he knew that this was his chance to let her go. But he wouldn't. He couldn't.

"I'm all in. We will deal with this together. I promise." Pearson could see the relief reflected in the depths of her ebony eyes, and he couldn't help but kiss her lips again.

Little did she know that he would do anything for her. Pearson was more than all in, he was head over heels.

"Great, I can call in a few favors and we can release a statement." Monique replied, but Pearson had a feeling that she still was uncertain about their plan.

It was okay. He had enough faith for both of them. Everything would work out just fine. He was no longer a trending topic, Darlene had crawled back under her rock, and his company's stocks were stable. Monique's plan had worked just like she said, and them being married was only one more positive check mark for him... for them both.

"I'm going to go to the bedroom, so I can call my mom and my office. And you need to go let your people know as well. I'm sure everyone will think we've both lost our minds." Monique chuckled, but it wasn't the light sound from earlier. It sounded uneasy and it made Pearson frown.

Monique was always sure. She always had a plan A, B, and C. And she had back-up plans for those. To know that she felt uncertain about them, made Pearson want to prove even more how right they were for one another.

"Okay, you make your calls, and I'll be out here, so I can make mine." Pearson forced a smile, and Monique returned a forced one of her own. He hated the gloomy feeling that had enveloped their romantic bubble.

Right then and there, Pearson promised himself that he would do everything in his power to always keep Monique happy. *No matter what.*

23

ALL OUT IN THE OPEN

"No, Mom, I didn't hurt you on purpose. I'm sorry you feel that way. No, he's a good man, mom. Yes, he's white. No I don't think he has any black people in his family." Monique sighed heavily while she rubbed her temple. *Sweet baby Jesus, I brought this on myself.*

"Mom, I have to go, okay? I'll be home in a few days and I promise you can ask me whatever you want. Yes, you can meet him then. Okay, bye mom. I love you." Monique quickly disconnected the phone as she sighed deeply.

"Lord Jesus, be an extra strength Tylenol. Because my nerves..." Monique said out loud as she flopped down on the large chaise lounge in the palatial bedroom.

Monique was really glad that the suite was huge, and that Pearson had stayed in the living area because her mother was on a roll. Her mother's guilt trip could put a nun to shame.

Monique already knew that she only had herself to blame, running off to Vegas and *accidently* getting married to a man her mother had never met, but damn she didn't mean to.

Monique didn't have the luxury or the time to worry about her mother though, because she had to do what she did best, and that was fix the situation. There wasn't anything negative being said about their marriage yet. However, Monique was well aware that that wouldn't last long. Monique knew that she would have to get in front of the story and spin it in a positive way, so that they could control the narrative.

This situation wasn't like when she first started working for Pearson. The damage had already been done, and she had to come in and rectify it, now however, she had the luxury this time to release a statement, and hold all the power. They didn't have to wait for someone else to tell their story, they could tell it themselves. And it would be the perfect Cinderella fairytale, the Brandy and Asian dude *Disney* version.

Monique continued to make the necessary calls to her office and the multitude of contacts that she knew would tell the story just the way she needed them to. Unlike previous situations where she would sweep her problems under the rug, this time, however, she would call in every favor she had to fix her personal life. *I can't let Pearson, or myself down.*

Once she finished making her business calls, she decided to finally call Venus. Since the story had broken on the gossip blogs, her phone had been blowing up. Her best friend didn't bother, so Monique knew she was pissed.

"Oh so, you *do* have my number," Venus answered on the first ring, and Monique smiled.

"Of course, I have your number. I love you! Plus, you're my very best friend and we go waaaay back like bobby socks and pigtails back." Monique's voice was as sweet as she could make it. She would use all the sugar she possessed to get her friend not to be upset.

"That's funny. You can remember that we go so far back. I mean I did beat up Bobby Middleton our freshman year because he talked about your outfit..."

"Hey, I was going to do it myself, you just beat me to it. Anyway, my outfit was fly. He deserved that ass whoopin." Monique interrupted but Venus continued as if she hadn't said a word.

"Yet, you told me a bold-face lie when you said you and *Mr. Grant* weren't married," Venus continued.

"Technically, I didn't tell a *bold-face* lie. I mean not intentionally." Monique grimaced.

"Explain. And don't leave anything out. Then I just might forgive you for robbing me of the pleasure of throwing you a raunchy bachelorette party with oiled-up strippers with swinging Mandingos."

Monique laughed out loud at her crazy friend. After arguing with her mother, answering her PA, Blake's a million and one questions, and practically groveling to get her story out the way she wanted it, she was glad to talk to someone that would always be on her side no matter what.

Monique told Venus all about her wild stay in Vegas. She started with her night of wedding bliss and ended with the foolishness of seeing Nikki and Damon together.

"I knew it was a reason I didn't like that bitch. What kind of trifling, good for nothing shit is that? She pretended to be your friend, and all the while she was sleeping with Damon." Venus sucked her teeth in disgust.

Monique shook her head; she couldn't believe the duplicity of both her former friend or her ex. It took a lot of balls to betray someone so close to you, and both of them did it without batting a lash. *Shameful.*

Even though Monique was glad that she and Damon had ended things, because it made room for Pearson, she still felt hurt that two people she was so close to wouldn't even consider her feelings.

"Yeah, well at least it's all out in the open, and I never have to deal with either of them again." Monique replied.

"Just so you know when I see that punk-ass Damon he's getting punched on sight. Just off principle." Venus had laughter in her voice, but Monique knew her friend was serious.

"Well, I won't stop you, as long as you don't stop me." Both women laughed, and Monique felt more like herself.

"So am I forgiven?" Monique asked already knowing the answer.

"Hell naw!" Venus responded, her tone harsh.

What the hell? Monique pulled the phone from her face and looked at it with a confused frown.

"What do you mean, hell naw?" Monique questioned, still frowning.

"Listen, I've been waiting on a reason to see Mr. Hardcore the long shlong stripper, and you took away my chance. I can't keep calling that man for private shows with only me there, he's going to start getting suspicious." Venus replied in a dry tone.

Monique couldn't help the laughter that burst from deep within her belly. It was all the pent up stress and anxiety that she had been feeling, coming out. Venus was truly a wonderful friend, and the craziest person she knew.

"Girl, if you were calling that man for private shows with just you, he was already suspicious," Monique said through her laughter.

Venus sucked her teeth again. "Whatever, heffah. I just hope your new husband isn't against a post wedding bachelorette party, because dammit, I need some ass shaking and ding dong slinging in my face. You just can't take that away from me."

"I'm sure Pearson will have a problem with a man's dick slinging in my face." Monique giggled.

"They don't have to be in your face. I mean dang, you got a husband already. Let your girl enjoy herself. Ole selfish ass," Venus mumbled the last part, but Monique heard her anyway.

"Whatever you plan will be fine, I'm sure," Monique said in a placating tone.

"Uh huh. But seriously, though. Moni, if you're happy... I'm happy for you." All traces of laughter were gone, and Monique could hear the sincerity in her best friend's voice.

Monique smiled, "Thank you, bestie. I am happy. Scared shitless, and a little out of my depth, but I'm happy."

"Okay, happy. Go get your groove on with your new husband, and I'll start planning the shindig."

As the women said their goodbyes, Monique couldn't help but be thankful for real friends that truly loved her.

~

MONIQUE AND PEARSON walked into the banquet hall dressed in their best. It was the last night of the conference, and the keynote speaker was set to hit the stage. They had been laying low since the news broke that they were married. She didn't know many of these people, but she still didn't want Pearson's networking opportunity to be over-shadowed by tabloid nonsense.

Pearson had been uptight since she told him that they couldn't skip the keynote speaker. The closer the time came for them to get dressed, the more silent and brooding he became. The tension was wrapped around them, and she hated it. Monique really wished Pearson would tell her what was really going on, *I hate secrets.*

Monique took a deep breath and tried to relax from the tension threating to swallow her whole. She glanced around as Pearson led her to their table. The holiday theme was obvious with the white lights and immaculate white table and chair coverings. The whole room looked like they were inside of a snow globe. It was the one thing to finally make her smile.

"Why are we so close to the damn stage?" Pearson mumbled in Monique's ear as he leaned down to pull out her chair. He scooted her under the table then took his seat next to her.

"You needed to be seen doing serious work. It's good for your image," Monique whispered through a fake smile that was plastered across her face.

Pearson had expressed how he hated the keynote speaker, Jeffery Mann, but he refused to divulge why he disliked the man so much, but knowing Pearson, it didn't take much for him not to like someone.

"This windbag is going to get his pompous ass on the stage and go on forever about how fucking great he is, I really could've missed this shit." Pearson's face held a neutral expression, but Monique could see in his eyes that he was more than a little agitated. She just didn't know why.

"What's going on with you? You know we can't just leave, Pearson. We're in the front of the stage with hundreds of your colleagues here.

It will look disrespectful and then *you* will be the pompous ass everyone will be talking about." Monique's tone was serious as she looked him in his eyes. They had come too far for him to show his ass now.

Pearson crossed his bulging arms over his chest defensively. "Fine. But for the record. These people don't mean shit to me, and I can do whatever the fuck I want," Pearson growled low, and Monique almost broke her neck she whipped it around so fast. She stared at the man who had the audacity to cuss at her.

"Who do you think you're talking to?" Monique questioned. Her face still held a smile for those looking on, but if anybody looked into her eyes they would see the fire burning within them.

Pearson turned his head to look in her direction. His face was a stony mask, but Monique knew that he was thinking carefully on his next words. But before he could say another word, Monique decided to give it to him straight with no chaser.

"In the past, you might've been able to do whatever the fuck *you* wanted, but we see where that got you. So now, you're going to do whatever the fuck *I* say. How 'bout that?!" Monique stared him down. She didn't know why he was in such a foul mood, but she'd be damned if she would take the brunt of his ire.

Pearson's face broke out into the most beautiful smile that Monique had ever witnessed on his face, and all she could do was stare. Not for the first time, Monique wondered if her husband was crazy. *Why the hell is he smiling, after talking to me crazy? He's out of his fine ass mind. What in the world have I gotten myself into?*

Monique stayed silent as Pearson moved closer to her. He slid his arm around the back of her chair, and rested his free hand on her thigh. She was glad that they had arrived early and were sitting at the table alone. Because when he leaned down and kissed her just beneath her ear, and moved his hand slowly up her leg, she couldn't help the shiver that raced through her body.

She couldn't control her body's reaction to him, but she wouldn't just give in to his manipulations. The last thing she wanted was to let him know just how sexy she thought he was while she was pissed.

"Gorgeous, I apologize if my words offended you. I would never speak to you in such a derogatory way ever. In general, you know that I do what the fuck I want, it's just who I am." Pearson kissed her cheek softly, and Monique wanted to swoon but she didn't. She cut her eyes at him and nodded stiffly.

There was no way she would be smooth talked into believing his bullshit. He was cussing at her, *and I'll be damned if a man talks to me any kind of way.*

"Monique." Pearson grabbed her chin gently, so that she would have to look at him. "I'm sorry, sweetheart. My words weren't directed toward you, honestly." His face was sincere and she was inclined to believe him, but Monique still needed to get her point across.

"Okay, but let me tell you this. Let that be the last time you cuss in my direction. Because I promise you won't like the outcome." Monique held his gaze as he nodded his understanding.

"Yes, ma'am." Pearson gave her a mock salute.

"You're already on thin ice, so don't get cute." Monique narrowed her eyes.

"I can't help the cuteness. I was born this way." Pearson smirked unapologetically.

Monique shook her head, she knew that the conversation would go nowhere with him trying to get on her good side, so she simply pursed her lips and turned away. She wasn't really all that upset, but she wouldn't be a doormat in this relationship. So he had to know that she was serious about her respect. *Hell, I've been disrespected enough, I'll be damned if I let my husband do it too.*

When three other men and two women joined them at their table, Monique made a conscious effort to relax, and Pearson started to talk to their table mates. He was even giving a semblance of a smile. Monique knew that he was trying for her sake, so she wouldn't make him suffer too much when they went back to their room *this time.*

24

FEAR AND LOATHING IN LAS VEGAS

Pearson knew that his wife was more than a little pissed off at him. Although she smiled and said all the right things while they sat at the elaborate decorated table, she was stiff and in work mode. *I hate fucking "work-mode" Monique.*

Pearson really wasn't cussing at his wife; fuck was just an everyday word to him. But considering Monique's reaction, he would definitely curve his usage of swear words around his gorgeous woman.

He looked toward the stage as Jeffery Mann was introduced. The loathing he felt seeing the man for the first time in years was indescribable. Although he told Dom that he didn't believe the man tried to kill him on the side of the road, Pearson still couldn't stand the older man.

Jeffery Mann was an evil son of a bitch and normally, Pearson wouldn't put it past him to do something so low. But everyone at the conference knew that Pearson was in attendance, including Mann, and there hadn't been anything untoward happen. So, Pearson's theory of Mann being the culprit behind his unfortunate accident didn't hold water.

As the man on the stage did exactly what Pearson said he would do, talk about himself, Pearson felt Monique shift closer to him. Usually that wouldn't mean much, whenever they were together they didn't seem to be more than a couple of inches apart, but Pearson knew that she was pissed at him, so he looked around to see what made his wife tense and move closer.

"You okay, gorgeous?" Pearson eyed the people at his table, but all of them were focused on the blowhard speaker, so he continued to look around the room.

"I'm fine." Monique said in what Pearson identified as her "professional" tone.

Pearson frowned and locked eyes with Monique. He could see the turmoil dancing through her beautiful brown irises, and he didn't like it one bit. It was crazy how they had only known each other for a small amount of time, but he could already tell so much about her.

"Sweetheart?" Pearson questioned seriously. He knew something was up, and he just wanted her to tell him so that he could fix it.

"Pearson, it's nothing. Can we just listen to the speaker please?" Monique's whispers were pleading, but he wouldn't drop it. The strain in her voice just made him want to know what was going on that much more.

"Monique, baby. I know that you're upset with me. I'll make it up to you I promise, but you just moved closer to me, and placed your arm underneath mine, and I know you're still pissed. So, what's going on?" Pearson whispered in her ear. He was doing his best not to attract attention, but like he said before, he really didn't give a fuck about what people thought. And he would do anything to get his wife to tell him what was wrong, even cause a scene.

Before she could answer his probing, movement from the other side of the room caught Pearson's attention. It was Damon and Nikki. They were holding hands and looking quite cozy as they made their way to their seats. Pearson didn't know much about the woman, Nikki, but he could tell by her demeanor that the late arrival for attention was probably her idea.

Pearson wasn't an insecure man by any means, but he had to ask his wife a few times if she was sure that she wasn't still in love with her ex. It wasn't like the two of them had a long courtship and then decided to elope. They got married on a whim, and hadn't even known each other for more than two months. Hell, their wedding night had been only their fourth date.

"If you want me to finish beating his ass, I will." Pearson wasn't joking at all. He hated to see the look of hurt that flashed across her heart-shaped face, plus that one punch didn't satisfy Pearson's urge to beat the shit out of Damon Hicks.

Monique gave him a slight smile and shook her head, "You are so quick to revert to violence." She ran her small hand down his face in a gentle caress, and he kissed the palm of her hand lovingly.

"You need to learn that I will do anything to see that beautiful smile grace your lips. And that asshole over there took it away, and I can't have that. Now, can I?" Pearson quirked an eyebrow in question, as Monique continued to shake her head. Her smile grew wider, though, and that's what Pearson really wanted.

"I couldn't ask for a better husband. But I need you to cool it down, Tarzan. We don't need you fighting." She looked around the room. "You especially can't fight here," Monique whispered but her eyes were alight with mirth, and he knew that the tension that was between them had melted away.

"Oh, come on. You don't want to be my Jane? I have a big ole' vine you can swing from anytime you want." Pearson winked at her. When Monique placed her hand over her mouth and ducked her head in laughter, he knew that he had gotten her to finally relax.

Pearson never knew that making anyone laugh could bring him so much joy. Hell, he never really thought about bringing anyone else joy before. *I'm glad I found her. My beautiful wife.*

Jeffery Mann continued to drone on and on, making the crowd delirious with boredom, but after another forty-five minutes of his nonsense, he finally sat down. Pearson was glad that the torture was finally over, so that he could get Monique back to their suite and make love to her all night before they had to leave the next day.

Pearson didn't like to feel cornered, and there were too many people he considered enemies in the room. He still needed to figure out who was trying to hurt him, or who leaked the information about his marriage to the press. Pearson knew that Monique was still in work mode trying to fix everything, but truth be told, now that the conference was over, so was her contract. Now, he would protect his wife. *And I dare someone to stand in my way.*

ALTHOUGH MONIQUE HAD RELAXED some since dinner, as Pearson walked with her small hand in his to their suite, he could still feel a slight tension between them. He needed to get her inside and solidify her forgiveness with his tongue on her body. However, Pearson's thoughts turned sour as they approached the hotel room door, because something felt off.

Although the door was shut, something just didn't feel right to Pearson. He entered the room slowly. Then he figured it out. There was no sound coming from the room, and the lights were out. When they left, Monique had made sure to turn on a couple of lamps and the TV. She said it was to make people think they were there, so they wouldn't break in.

"Hold on, baby. I want you to stay out here." Pearson stopped Monique from going into the room.

"What's wrong?" Monique questioned with a furrowed brow.

"The lights and the TV are turned off," Pearson said by way of explanation.

"Should I call security?" Monique's expression changed from confusion to worry in a blink of an eye.

"No, don't call yet. Let me check it out first." Pearson peered into the dark room.

"What if they're still in there?" Monique whispered frantically.

"It will be fine, sweetheart. I promise." Pearson quickly pecked the tip of Monique's nose reassuringly and quietly entered the suite.

Pearson looked around slowly. He took his phone from his suit pocket, and used it to light a path around the room. The space was large, but as his eyes adjusted to the darkness he noticed there wasn't anybody in the living area, and nothing seemed out of place. He relaxed slightly, but then he heard movement in the bedroom. He started to move stealthily toward the room when he heard Monique enter behind him. He sighed heavily.

"I told you to wait outside," Pearson whispered angrily. Somebody was indeed in the room, and if he had to fight, he didn't want to worry about Monique's safety.

"You were taking too long. I was worried," Monique whispered back with her hand on her hips and her lips pursed.

Pearson nodded toward the closed bedroom door then placed his finger against his lips to motion for Monique to stop talking. She nodded her understanding, and they headed toward the bedroom door.

Pearson cracked the door open quietly. He held out his hand for Monique to stay put, and then he entered the room. He spotted the tall shadowy figure hovering over the safe. Pearson instantly felt rage like he had never felt before.

How dare someone break in to his space and try to steal from him. Not only that, but he had violated a place where his wife laid her head, and there wasn't any way in hell he was going to let that shit slide.

In a flash, Pearson was standing behind the crouching man. The man didn't even hear him coming; Pearson quickly slipped his arm around the man's neck and had him in an unbreakable choke hold.

The man began to struggle, but Pearson began to tighten his arm. Pearson wasn't a muscle bound guy, but he did work out, and it was his undeniable fury that fueled his aggression.

"Who the fuck are you?" Pearson growled pushing his arm into the man's throat.

The man coughed but didn't answer as he grasped at Pearson's tightening arm.

"Answer me, asshole! I will kill you right the fuck now!" Pearson yelled, his patience was gone. If the fucker didn't answer his questions, he was of no use anyway... *so I might as well kill his ass.*

"I-I...I'm just do... do doin' a job," the man choked out through gasps. Pearson loosened his hold slightly so that the man could speak.

"What job? Who the fuck sent you?" Pearson questioned, his anger growing by every second.

"I- I... don't know..." Pearson had heard enough of the stuttering excuses. He tightened his grip once more until the man passed out.

Before Pearson could further inspect the room, he was blinded by the lights being abruptly turned on.

"Mr. Grant?! Is everything okay?" One of the three security guards yelled as they rushed into the room.

Pearson was still pissed, but he wasn't even breathing hard after choking a man into unconsciousness.

"I'm just great, except for the fact an intruder was in my mother-fucking suite where he could've hurt my wife!" Pearson's voice grew louder with each word.

"We will take care of it, sir," the same guard responded, kneeling over the intruder.

With the lights on, Pearson could clearly see the man's face, and unfortunately, he had no idea who the man was. It could've just been a coincidence that some random guy had broken into his hotel suite, or someone was really out to get Pearson.

"I need to speak to the head of security now!" Pearson left the guards to handle the sleeping intruder as he went in search of his wife. He knew that Monique must've called security when he left her outside of the bedroom.

Pearson found her pacing in the living room, biting her nails. He quirked his head to the side as he watched her. He had seen a lot of her nervous habits, but never nail biting. Pearson could tell that she was worried to death, and he hated to see her like that. However, she was still the epitome of beauty, still wearing her long crimson and black evening gown.

"Hey, are you okay, beautiful?" Pearson asked walking closer to her. Monique was so distracted that he could tell she hadn't heard him approach.

Monique threw her arms around his neck and held him tight.

Pearson wrapped his arms around her waist and pulled her as close to his body as he could. She melted into his embrace, and Pearson knew that she was where she belonged.

"Am I okay? Are *you* okay? I heard you yelling, but when I peeked inside I saw that you had the upper hand so I called security." She rushed out, still holding his neck tightly.

Pearson loosened her arms from around his neck and stepped back slightly, so he could see her face. Her tears had spilled from her eyes and down her cheeks, and the sight of her crying wrecked his soul.

As Pearson continued to hold Monique as she cried, the security team led the intruder out of the room in handcuffs. The lead security guard told Pearson before he left, that the head of safety and security for the hotel would be there shortly to ask them some questions.

Pearson felt Monique shudder as she sniffled.

"I'm fine, baby. I promise," Pearson reassured her, as he wiped the tears from her face.

"How the hell did he even get in here?" Monique questioned her eyes welling up with more tears.

"I don't know, but I'm going to find out. Go pack your bags. We are getting the fuck out of here *tonight*."

Pearson would answer the head of the hotel's security's questions, and he would ask a few of his own. However, Pearson knew he had to contact the one guy that could get to the bottom of all the bullshit quickly.

When Monique left to go pack, Pearson pulled out his phone. He noticed for the first time that he had a few voicemails and missed calls from Keifer and Mark. *I'll deal with them later.*

"Hello?" the deep brooding voice answered after the third ring.

"Dom. I have a problem."

25

IT ALL FALLS DOWN

Monique was beyond frustrated with her new husband. He had been making phone calls since he'd told her to pack. Now, they were headed to the airport to fly back to Dallas because of a break in at their suite.

She had a feeling that something more was going on and she hated to be kept in the dark. Pearson was brooding while he snapped and hollered at whoever was on the other end of the line, and all Monique could do was shake her head at him. She would find out soon enough what was going on, but for now, she would ear hustle his side of the conversation.

"We'll be on a flight in less than thirty minutes. I need all the information you can find out about Ray Turner. Yeah, *everything*. I want to know how many times his ass goes to the toilet," Pearson growled angrily.

Monique licked her lips as she watched Pearson. She knew it was crazy to find his behavior sexy. She was over feeling guilty about wanting this man. He was her husband now, and even though their relationship didn't start conventionally, she would still put her all into them. She wanted their relationship to work, she wanted to be happy, and she wanted love.

When Pearson turned his attention toward her, she couldn't help the smile that graced her lips. The man could make her blood boil with just a look. And his eyes were saying all kinds of naughty things.

He took her hand in his, raised it to his lips, and kissed her palm. *I'm falling for my husband. I guess crazier things have happened.*

Pearson turned back to his phone call, so Monique decided to check her phone for any updates. She was able to release her version of their whirlwind romance on several different blogs, social media sites, and entertainment news outlets. Once the story was out, the clamoring for their story died down considerably.

As a matter of fact, Pearson or their cyclone nuptials weren't even a trending topic anymore. Thanks to two C-list celebrities getting into a fight live on social media, Pearson and Monique's news fell into the oblivion.

Pearson finally ended his call when they pulled up to a private airstrip. Monique peeked out the window in shock. It was one thing to fly first class, but it was a whole other level to fly private. She knew that Pearson was rich, but she didn't realize he was *rich, rich.*

"Are we flying on a private jet?" Monique still couldn't quite believe what she was seeing. She'd just assumed they had gotten last-minute tickets on a commercial flight.

"Yes. We could've flown here on my jet, but it would've taken too much to get us here on such short notice."

"So, leaving tonight isn't short notice?" Monique questioned seriously. *Who the hell am I really married to?*

"No, we were scheduled to leave tomorrow morning, but the plane was already here. It took some finagling to change the flight time and plans, but there's nothing money can't buy." Pearson winked at her and Monique's core tightened in response. There was nothing like being with a boss, and Pearson was definitely that.

Monique could feel the tension rolling off of Pearson as he sat brooding in his seat, and she really needed to get down to what the hell was going on with him.

"So are you going to sit and sulk the entire flight or are you going to tell me what's going on?" Monique asked when they had settled into their flight.

"I'm a grown ass man. I don't sulk, Monique," Pearson replied *sulkily*.

Monique smirked. He never called her by her name. It was always beautiful or gorgeous. He even called her Moni, but never her full name.

"Uh-huh. Listen, we've dealt with enough shit already, so let's not go through the rigmarole that nothing is wrong or that I shouldn't worry about anything. We are a team now, so just tell me what's up," Monique snapped before he could even fix his lips to lie.

Pearson sighed heavily like he had the weight of the world on his shoulders, and Monique prepared herself for the worst.

"I think someone is trying to kill me." His words were so smooth and came out so nonchalantly that Monique almost missed the meaning.

"Wait. What the hell are you talking about?" Monique unbuckled her seatbelt and scooted up in her seat to get a closer look at his face.

Pearson was worried. His face was lined in anxiousness. Monique was so focused on his anger that she missed the worry underneath.

Pearson unbuckled his seatbelt and motioned for her to take a seat on his lap. Monique went to him without any hesitation, wrapping her arms around his neck. She had a feeling that they both needed comforting. Pearson tightened his hold around Monique's waist, and she held his neck just a tight.

"The accident on the side of the road wasn't an accident. There weren't any skid marks to indicate the driver had tried to slow down or even swerve to keep from hitting me. The investigators I hired told me that. The police just thought it was an accident and didn't investigate it thoroughly."

"What else happened?" Monique was surprised that she'd managed to keep her voice calm, steady even.

"Besides all of the leaks to the press, my downtown apartment was broken into this week while I was away, the board of directors tried to have a secret meeting about my company without me there."

Monique couldn't believe all of the stuff that he had been keeping from her. *Damn I hopped right out the frying pan and into the fire.*

"Do you know who is behind any of this?" she questioned her voice still calm.

"With the stunt that'd just been pulled with the board of directors, I have my suspicions. I'm just waiting on confirmation." Pearson kissed the top of her head and she snuggled closer to him.

They were having a ridiculous conversation about setups, killing, and corporate takeovers, and she was sitting in his lap. The bad thing about it all was it felt normal. Maybe it was a good thing. After all, they were a married couple. Their instant closeness just helped to solidify their relationship.

"When we get home, I want you to live with me." Pearson switched the topic so fast, her head began to spin. Monique normally would argue about living together so soon, but hell, they were already married, and she honestly didn't want to sleep without him.

"Okay." Monique looked up into his shocked expression and she couldn't help but laugh.

"Okay? Just like that? I just knew that I would have to bribe you or knock you over the head and drag you back to my cave," Pearson said on a chuckle, the light slightly returning to his eyes.

"I'm not going to fight about trivial things with you. We're a married couple and apparently, you have a price on your head, so I might as well live with you to keep you in line." Monique smiled, but it was shaky. She was scared out of her mind to venture into the real world as husband and wife. Everything had been fine and dandy in Vegas where they were living in their own little world, not having to answer to others. But now they would be cohabitating and sharing in one another's lives. Monique was terrified of failing and even more so in this relationship.

"I'm glad you're so agreeable because you will also have twenty-four-hour security with you until Dom clears all this shit up."

"Security?" Monique frowned at the idea of someone following her around all day, but with two break-ins and a rogue driver, she didn't want to take any chances. "Okay," she conceded after a second.

"Good." Pearson kissed her lips, but the kiss soon turned heated.

"Where did the flight attendant go?" Monique asked through frantic kisses.

"He knows not to come back into the cabin unless we call him." Pearson was untucking her shirt from her jeans, and Monique's hips had a mind of their own as they started grinding against his cock that was starting to harden under her movements.

"Are you going to introduce me to the mile-high club?" Monique asked, her hips still swiveling and grinding.

"You're damn right I am." Pearson had her stripped down to nothing in no time at all.

Monique would've been completely embarrassed by the loud screams she made if she'd actually given a damn. But Pearson was dicking her down so good, she didn't have a care in the world.

"ARE YOU READY, BEAUTIFUL?" Pearson's arms were wrapped around her from behind, and Monique leaned her head back on his muscular chest.

"Are *you* ready? I mean with the stuff with your business, we can postpone meeting my mom to another time."

Pearson chuckled, and Monique frowned. "What's so funny?"

"You can try and pretend that my business is the reason you want to postpone me meeting your mom, but you know you're just putting off the inevitable. I'm your husband and I'm not going anywhere." Pearson turned Monique around and pecked her pouting lips.

Monique huffed. "I just don't know how she's going to act and my whole entire family is going to show up being nosey. And then there's Ashley..."

Although Monique was now aware that it was Nikki cheating with Damon, her sister still tended to act inappropriately around Monique's dates, and the last thing she needed was another fight with her sister. She just wished they could've stayed in their blissful Vegas love bubble because the real world sucked salty balls.

"Everything will be just fine. It's me and you. Period," Pearson answered.

"Well, let's get this circus moving." Monique grimaced.

Twenty-five minutes later, they were pulled up to Monique's mother's home. Just as she predicted, there was a line of cars parked outside. Monique rolled her eyes heavenward. *Nosey asses...*

Monique and Pearson parked and made their way inside the crowded house. It was like it was the holidays, except Christmas had been the week before.

"Hey, there's my wayward child," Mrs. Carter said as she opened the door.

It took everything in Monique not to suck her teeth, but she managed to put on the widest and fakest smile she could muster.

"Hi, Mama. This is Pearson Grant," Monique introduced, ignoring her mother's shade.

"Mrs. Carter, it's nice to meet you." Pearson's deep voice rumbled as he took her hand and kissed it.

Mrs. Carter ate up the attention, blushing and batting her eyelashes like a school girl.

"Well, aren't you handsome... ya'll come on in and sit down. The food is almost ready."

Monique nodded as they made their way deeper inside the house. She introduced Pearson to some of the family, bypassing others with their screwed-up faces. She didn't need any shit from anyone, including family. They took their seats at the dining room table. Monique was a little relieved at the easy conversation Pearson was having with most everyone.

Even her mom had stopped making little comments and had settled into a civil conversation with Pearson. Everything was going pretty good, and Monique was almost able to breathe a sigh of relief until her younger sister sauntered into the house.

Monique knew she had to apologize to her sibling for thinking the worst of her, but she felt nervous about talking to Ashley because of their strenuous relationship.

"Well, if it isn't Mr. and Mrs. Grant. I'm surprised to see you here slumming it with us plain folks." Ashley sneered.

Monique was so over her sister. It was an endless circle of nonsense and ghettoness. Her sister would say something ignorant, and Monique would threaten to kick her ass, and on and on. *Not today, Satan.*

"Ashley, can I talk to you in the kitchen for a minute?" Monique asked, getting out of her chair and heading into the kitchen. She knew that her sister would follow because she lived for the drama. But this wasn't about the dramatics. Monique actually wanted to put all of their tension behind them.

Monique heard Ashley suck her teeth, but she was right. Her sister followed her into the kitchen.

"What?" Ashley snapped, her hands going to her hips with attitude.

"I just want to apologize to you. I'm sorry for thinking the worst of you without proof. You are family, and I should've been woman enough to come to you. I'm truly sorry," Monique stated sincerely. Even though Ashley had insinuated more than once that Damon wanted her, Monique should've just asked her sister instead of assuming the worst.

"What the fuck are you talking about?" Ashley's face was screwed into an angry mask.

Monique sighed. She knew this wouldn't be easy, but she would be a woman about it and suck down her prideful retorts and do what needed to be done.

"I thought you were sleeping with Damon behind my back, but I found out it wasn't true when I saw him and Nikki cozied up in Vegas together. The whole time we were together, he was sleeping with my so-called friend," Monique admitted humbly, shaking her head at her own foolishness.

Ashley's face remained in an angry sneer. "What the hell do you mean Damon is sleeping with Nikki?"

"I know. I couldn't believe it either," Monique said, still shaking her head without noticing her sister's reaction.

"You saw them together?" Ashley seemed to be more than a little confused.

Monique frowned. "Uh, yeah. They were in Vegas *together*." Monique cocked an eyebrow at her sister.

"That sneaky motherfucker! He told me he wasn't fucking that bitch. After all this time, me waiting for him to leave you, and him promising I was the only one! I knew I couldn't trust his dog ass. I can't wait to catch his bitch ass." Ashley was so distracted, cursing Damon's name with her loud ranting that she hadn't realized that she had let her little secret slip.

"You backstabbing bitch!" Monique lunged at her sister and all hell broke loose.

26

ENEMY AMONG US

P earson couldn't help but move closer to the kitchen when Monique led her sister there to talk. He didn't interrupt them, but he stood close by just in case. He knew that the two women had problems that ran pretty deep, and although Monique didn't elaborate on everything that had happened between them, Pearson could feel the tension every time the two siblings were in the same room.

When he heard the crazy ranting of Ashley, Pearson knew the shit was about to hit the fan. He couldn't believe that sneaky asshole was not only sleeping with Nikki but Ashley as well. Pearson shook his head, at least the pictures were only of Nikki. Pearson wouldn't have been able to keep his mouth shut if he'd known about Ashley.

"You backstabbing bitch!" Pearson entered the kitchen just as Monique lunged at her sister, punching her in the jaw.

Ashley stumbled back, losing her footing. She fell to the floor with a thud. Monique jumped on top of her and punched her again. Ashley was able to buck Monique off of her, and the two women were in an all-out WWE style brawl. Pearson stood stunned for a minute before Ashley's screeching broke him out of his daze.

He pulled Monique off of her sister as their family seemed to finally make their way into the kitchen to see what was going on. Monique's mother ran in with wide eyes, staring at her two daughters.

Pearson was trying to calm Monique down while another guy, who Pearson thought was a cousin, had a hold of Ashley.

"Monique? What in the world are you doing? I can't believe you're acting like this. I didn't raise you to be this way!" Mrs. Carter had finally regained her ability to speak rushed to Ashley's side as she chastised Monique as if she were a child.

Pearson frowned at the woman. She'd only addressed Monique and not Ashley. She was acting as if Monique wasn't justified in hitting her sister.

Monique stopped trying to get out of Pearson's hold and immediately started to take deep breaths. It was as if all the fight had left her. Her eyes that were so full of anger just seconds before were now swimming with sadness. The sight broke Pearson's heart.

"Mama," Monique started calmly, taking another deep breath. "I am disappointed that my only *sister* was sleeping with *my* boyfriend while we were together." Monique had stressed the two words, sneering at her sister.

Mrs. Carter waved her hand like Monique's words were foolish. "You're not even with that boy anymore. You're married to this white boy now, so why does it even matter if your sister dated him?"

Pearson couldn't believe what he was hearing. *What the fuck kind of backward ass thinking is that?*

Monique shook her head, "No mama, she wasn't dating him; she was screwing him behind my back. What matters is that my whore of a sister slept with the man *I* was dating."

"You better watch your mouth, little girl." Mrs. Carter sneered, and Pearson was ready to pull Monique to his car and never come back.

"I told you the last time we had this discussion that I was tired of putting up with all this bullshit. I was ready to put the past behind us and I even apologized," she spoke to both her mother and sister. "But neither of you are satisfied. You don't want to see me happy, you can't

stand to see me win. So neither one of ya'll have to see me again."
Monique's words were so cold that they sent a shiver down his spine.

"Pearson, get me the fuck out of here," Monique stated with
finality.

"Okay. Come on, baby, let's go home. We can deal with this later,"
Pearson consoled, holding Monique's hand as they began to
walk away.

"You always thought you were better than me, that's why I fucked
your man." Ashley cackled, holding her swelling eye as they were
leaving.

Monique whirled around and shouted back, "No, *you know* that
I'm better than you, and that's why you fucked him. But that's fine
little sister. You will always be the sad, pathetic bitch that had to go
behind her sister for sloppy seconds because she wasn't good enough
to find her own man."

~

THE ENTIRE CAR ride was filled with uncomfortable silence. The
tension was rolling off of Monique and she was trembling with what
Pearson could only figure was anger. He had never witnessed
anything like that in his life. His parents were both gone and he didn't
have any siblings, and his aunt, uncle, and his cousin, Kelsey, were
the only immediate family he had. And they were pretty low key, so
dysfunctional family gatherings weren't something he had ever experienced.

Once they made it back to his gated community, Pearson knew
that it was time to address the craziness. After they made their way
inside of the immaculate estate, they settled in the living room to talk.

"Interesting turn of events." Pearson's deep voice finally broke the
silence.

"You didn't know you married a hood chick, huh?"

He could tell that Monique was disappointed in herself, but
Pearson understood. There was no way anybody should be able to
betray you in such a way and just get away with it. "I don't believe it

was *hood* for you to fight your sister who committed the ultimate betrayal." Pearson shrugged. "I think she deserved that ass kicking. There's nothing hood about that, baby."

"I just felt so guilty for thinking that my sister could do that to me. Then I felt relieved that it was Nikki, even though she was my friend. I thought... at least it wasn't my sister. But it turned out to be *both*." Monique laughed.

Pearson nodded, "I'm sorry that you had to go through all of this."

"Thanks. But at least I know now. Can you do me a favor?"

"Anything," Pearson said without hesitation.

"Make love to me so I can forget. I just want to be lost in you." Monique's eyes were pleading and she would never have to beg him for anything.

Pearson didn't say anything else, he simply scooped her into his arms and carried her to the master bedroom.

He undressed her slowly, rubbing his large hands all over her silky, smooth skin. Pearson kissed and caressed every dip and valley that her succulent body had to offer. He nuzzled his face between her spread legs. Inhaling the womanly aroma of her arousal. Pearson stuck out his tongue, lightly licking her swollen lips through her soaking wet panties.

Monique moaned loudly, her hips thrusting upward, seeking more of his tongue. Pearson loved when she did that; her body moving without conscious thought. It was like he was a musician and her body was the instrument that played his every sensual tune.

Pearson slipped her panties from her body and licked her pussy with a voraciousness that couldn't be contained. Monique's body began to hum with her emerging orgasm as Pearson continued to lap and lick at her sweetness.

"Fuck me, Pear. I need you, baby," Monique groaned as she pulled at his hair.

Those words, her body, and the taste of her on his tongue made Pearson hard as stone. He could barely get his pants down before he was pushing inside of his wife.

He stilled as soon as he pushed deep inside of her pulsating pussy. The feeling was like no other, and he was barely holding on to his sanity. *Heaven.*

Monique pushed her hips upward, and that was all it took for Pearson to move. He pushed into her wet canal, hitting her sugary walls with every stroke. He moved up just enough to get his hand between them, and rubbed her clit in a tight circular motion. He felt the tell-flutters and he knew that she was close. Pearson knew that Monique didn't want slow and sensual, she wanted hard and fast to make her forget. And that's exactly what he would give her.

"Cum for your husband, gorgeous. I can feel your pussy flutter. I know you want to," Pearson whispered hoarsely into Monique's ear as she moaned her release.

Monique's legs shook and her body trembled with her orgasm, but Pearson didn't stop. He flipped her over and began pounding her still quivering pussy from behind. He slapped her juicy ass and watched it bounce back on his hard cock.

The sight alone could make him cum, but he wasn't ready yet. He wanted to make it last. He wanted to help his wife to forget her troubles. Hell, he wanted to forget his too.

"I'm going to cum again! Don't stop. Shit! Fuck! Please! Don't stop!" Monique screamed profanities as she bounced her fat ass back against his six pack.

Pearson leaned over, putting his chest to her back while still grinding into her pussy. He reached around to rub her clit once more, and Monique exploded. This time, there was no holding back. Pearson let go and shot every bit of himself deep inside of his wife.

"Fuck, I love you." Pearson breathed as he rolled off Monique, trying not to smother her with his big body.

"And I love you," Monique replied sleepily.

Pearson smiled because just like that, they had admitted their love. No big productions or grand announcements, just a simple "I love you." Pearson wished everything could be as simple, but he knew that was just wishful thinking.

～

THE NEXT MORNING CAME QUICKLY, and before he knew it, Pearson was en route to his office to head off the perceived takeover by someone he thought he could trust. If it weren't for Kelsey overhearing the sly bastard, Pearson would have still been in Vegas, completely unaware of the enemy that had been so close to him that he'd considered him a friend.

Pearson went through his private entrance through the garage of the building to get to his office. He didn't want any of the snakes to see him entering through the lobby and ruin his element of surprise.

"I knew you were going to be here bright and early." Kelsey smiled deviously as soon as Pearson exited his private elevator he hardly ever used.

He returned her devious smile with one of his own. There was a reason he kept it a secret that he and Kelsey were related. People tended not to watch what they did and said when the boss wasn't around. And with Kelsey's efficient and cool demeanor, nobody would ever suspect that she was his eyes and ears while he was out of the office. That's how he knew what the assholes were planning while he was away. If it weren't for Kelsey, Pearson would've been too late to stop their so-called takeover.

"What time will Dom be here?" Pearson asked as he continued to walk down the vacant hallway located in the back of his office.

"He's already waiting in your office." Kelsey nodded with a wink.

"I should've known his ass would beat me here. Make sure my personal attorney will be here on time and alert security to be ready to escort these assholes off my property when it's time." Pearson was in go mode and he was ready to cut the heads off all the snakes that were in his midst.

Pearson had left Monique curled up under the covers, sleeping peacefully. He knew that she wanted to be with him today for support, but after the stressful events of the previous night, he didn't want her anywhere near the cluster fuck that was about to take place.

"I'm glad that I can count on you," Pearson stated as soon as he entered his office.

Dom's dark head was bowed, engaged in his phone while his feet were propped up on the conference table.

Dom nodded his head. The man almost never smiled, so Pearson wasn't surprised at the blank expression on his face but the twinkle in his blue eyes conveyed his excitement about what was about to go down.

"You know I wouldn't miss this shit. I'm a man of my word and I told you if that son of a bitch ever tried anything, I wouldn't hesitate to take care of his ass."

"Well, I don't need you to take care of him per se. Well I don't at this moment." Pearson smirked.

"Yeah, well, the asshole has it coming. So whatever you give him, he deserves," Dom answered seriously still not smiling.

The next hour was spent going over all the evidence Dom had been able to collect on the saboteurs. They were thoroughly prepared to bury the asshole that dared to cross Pearson Grant.

When the board members, all of the directors, and his vice president were in the board room sitting nice and comfortable, Pearson and Dom made their way in with security trailing them.

The looks of fear and disbelief ran rampant over the faces of the backstabbers in the room while others just held confusion over Pearson being back from his "vacation" so soon.

"I thought you were in Vegas?"

"That's what I wanted you to think. I needed to weed out the enemies in my boardroom," Pearson responded his eyes narrowed.

"Pearson, now just wait a minute."

"Mark, you're fired." Pearson looked directly at his vice president. He couldn't believe the man that he had trusted for the last five years as his right hand was behind everything. The news of his marriage, the man trying to run him over, he even paid Darlene to be aggressive in the interview to get Pearson to flip out.

Mark Simon was trying to make Pearson look so incompetent that the board of directors would agree to turn over the reins to him. Mark needed to be in control so that he could up the ante on his insider trading. Mark had gotten in way over his head and owed a lot of bad people a lot of money, the only reason his plan started to fall apart was because he got greedy and started taking too many risks.

In October, when time started winding down and his debts started piling up, Mark started his plan of sabotage and takeover. If Monique hadn't been there to help him out of the first shit storm, there never would've been an attempt on his life. But with all greedy bastards, they start to get careless, and Dom was able to follow the money right to Mark Simon.

Fucking snake!

Mark and two of his board member buddies were escorted out of the building and into the waiting arms of law enforcement. And Pearson was finally able to breathe easier.

27

MOVING ON

When Monique woke the next morning and found Pearson gone, she knew that he was trying to protect her from all of the shit that was happening at his company. The night before, he had told her bluntly that she was officially fired. Pearson didn't want her to feel obligated to keep finding solutions to all his problems, and she understood. But she still wished he would've let her help him.

Once everything had gone down at his office, he called her and let her know all of the details. It was simply amazing that people could betray you so easily. Hell, she was still reeling from the fact that her friend and her sister were both sleeping with her man. And neither of them felt any sort of remorse.

Monique wasn't the type of woman to feel sorry for herself, but damn, those hits were like punches to the throat. It was something that she'd never expected and it caught her completely off guard. But what made it even worse was her mother. She couldn't believe the things her mother had said to her. She blamed Monique for everything, and she just didn't understand it.

"I'm done with the dysfunction. I will pray and probably even go to therapy, but I refuse to do this shit anymore," Monique said as she got ready for her day.

She was sipping a cup of coffee when her phone went off with several notifications.

"Aww hell." She didn't even want to look, but she knew she had to. The headlines were shocking even though she knew it was coming.

Pearson Grant's VP Arrested on Attempted Murder Charges

Vice President Tries to Kill his Way into Power

Mark Simon, Killer VP.

Monique would never underestimate the power of the press or their ability to rush to get the story to the masses. When there was a knock at the door, Monique smiled because she knew that it was Venus. Her best friend has just gotten back in town and with everything that had gone down, it was a must that they get together.

"Chiiile," Venus said as soon as Monique opened the door.

"Girl, I already know," Monique responded, shaking her head as she led Venus into the massive kitchen.

Once Venus settled on a stool with her own cup of coffee, Monique began the tale of ridiculousness that was her life.

"Girl! I cannot believe your sister is that damn trifling. I mean I can, but damn." Venus' mouth was hanging open in disbelief.

"I can't believe my mama blamed me for whoopin' her ass." Monique sipped her coffee, but it left a bitter taste in her mouth or maybe it was the subject.

"You know your mom has always favored Ashley. Let's just be honest, but I really am surprised about how she behaved," Venus replied with a frown.

"I understand why she babied Ashley, but the way she treated me yesterday..." Monique trailed off.

"Listen, Ashley was lied to when ya'll were kids, and she had the right to be upset with your mother, but..." Venus shrugged, and Monique nodded in agreement.

When they were younger, Monique's mother didn't tell Ashley who her real father was. Monique's father passed away when the girls were ten and twelve years old. Mr. Carter had adopted Ashley and they'd never told her that she was a product of an affair. When a loud mouth relative told Ashley she wasn't a "real" Carter, all hell broke loose, and their mother had been babying her since.

"Yes, Ashley had the right to be upset with my mother, not *me*. And Mama had no right whatsoever to treat me the way she has. It's not my fault Ashley is a damned side baby. I never said a word or treated her like she was."

"Girl, I think you just need to let go and let God at this point. Your mama never forgave herself, and I don't know why the blame shifted to you, but obviously, at some point it did." Venus' voice softened with her observation, but Monique knew her friend was speaking nothing but the truth.

Monique sighed, "I think I'll do just that... let God handle it. I was thinking about even going to therapy. I don't want this to fuck up my future relationships."

"I think that's a great idea," Venus responded with a smile.

"Thanks for being here. There's nothing like coming home to introduce your new husband to your dysfunctional ass family and having an all-out smack down with your sister." Monique chuckled.

"He might as well get used to the foolishness now." Venus chuckled, and Monique agreed.

The women finished their coffee and conversation, and Monique felt a million times better. The fallout that happened with her family was inevitable, but she hated that it had to go down the way that it did. The animosity and pettiness that Ashley often displayed was nothing compared to the duplicity. Monique knew that her sister was jealous, but she had no idea that Ashley hated her.

Monique always claimed that she would just move on, but this time, she was serious. After last night's debacle, it wasn't good for her soul to stay around people who meant her harm both mentally and physically. It was really and truly time to just move on. Family or not, it was time to cut ties.

∾

"Gᴏʀɢᴇᴏᴜs, I'ᴍ ʜᴏᴍᴇ." Pearson yelled from down stairs.

Monique smiled at the ease of their routine already. It had been a few weeks since they had gotten back from Vegas, and Pearson had already arranged for movers to pack up her house and bring all of her things to their home in Highland Village.

Monique decided not to put her house on the market, and just rent it out for the time being. Dealing with their whirlwind romance, all of the mess with Pearson's company, and Mark Simon's trial, she didn't want to deal with selling a house on top of all that.

"I'm in the bedroom!" she hollered back.

Monique continued to unpack her bags when she heard him come into the bedroom. She had to admit that the closet in their master bedroom was a dream. It was essentially another bedroom and it even had a sitting area. Hell, it was so large that she didn't even have enough clothes to fill up her side.

"Hey, wife. You've gotten quite a bit accomplished in here." Pearson's loving face made Monique smile.

The more they got to know each other, the more that she knew that their marriage was meant to be. *They* were meant to be.

"Yeah, it's amazing what I can get done when you're not here to distract me." She smirked at him.

Pearson shrugged unapologetically. "Beautiful, I won't apologize for wanting my hot as fuck wife. I mean come on. Look at you." Pearson gave her a once over then licked his lips longingly, and Monique could feel herself getting turned on.

"Damn, now I'm hard. What are you going to do about that Mrs. Grant?" Pearson sauntered closer to her, and before she could even pretend that she wanted to protest, he pounced.

Pearson kissed her deeply, and just like every other time that he touched her, Monique melted. If there was one thing that Monique loved, it was getting lost in her husband's kisses.

"Ummm, there you go distracting me again." Monique giggled as Pearson ran his hands down her ribs.

"Oh, baby, I have a huge distraction waiting just for you." Pearson winked as he started to remove his clothing in a slow strip tease.

Monique giggled again when he started humming and gyrating his hips.

"You are so crazy." Monique laughed when he threw his shirt over his head.

"Crazy for you, gorgeous." Pearson smiled.

"And corny, you're both crazy and corny." Monique chuckled.

"Oh… you wound me, wife. How could you call me corny? Just for that, you're about to take all this "corny" cock! With a spanking on the side." Pearson growled, as he flipped Monique over on her stomach and slapped her ass hard.

However, the sting of his slap only turned her on more, so all she could do was moan out her pleasure. Monique felt the heat of his large body hovering over her back as Pearson's tongue made a hot trail from her shoulder blades down to the cheeks of her ass. He bit each one playfully before slapping her ass once more. Then nothing.

"Pear?" Pearson had stopped moving. Monique felt the warmth of his body disappear. "Pearson?" Monique went to turn over to see why her husband had suddenly left her high and dry. *Well I'm not exactly dry,* Monique turned over ready to give Pearson some major attitude.

She turned over in a huff and sat up only to stop before an angry retort could leave her lips. Tears sprung to her eyes as she looked at her husband kneeling on the floor beside their bed with a ring box in his hand.

"Monique, from the first time that I laid eyes on you when you walked into my conference room and I acted like a total pervert…" Monique chuckled before Pearson continued with a smirk.

"I couldn't take my eyes off of you, and you have been on my mind ever since. I couldn't wait to make you my wife, and now that you are, I can't wait to see you walk down the aisle to say you will be mine forever. Will you do me the honor of being my wife?"

Monique's smile was huge in spite of the tears spilling down her face, she never would've thought that her life would've changed so drastically when she agreed to fix Pearson Grant's reputation.

"I'm already your wife." Monique's teary laugh sounded throughout the room.

"Yes, but you're not wearing my ring." Pearson slowly opened the ring box he held.

The ring was miraculous. Monique had never seen anything like it before in her life. The diamond was a halo set in a cushion cut surrounded by a double row of smaller diamonds lining each side of the ring.

"Oh my God! Pearson, it's beautiful!" Monique's eyes were wide as he slipped the magnificent piece of jewelry on her finger. It was a perfect fit.

"I love you," they said in unison, laughed, and then kissed.

"Well, it looks like I have a wedding to plan." Monique smiled as she wiped away her happy tears.

"Yep, just tell me the place and time and I'll be there." Pearson smiled in return.

"Great! And Venus will be happy she'll get to plan my bachelorette party." Monique smiled widely, knowing that comment would get Pearson back for his earlier teasing.

"Venus already told me about her obsession with the stripper, so her planning your party will have to be a strong hell no from your husband." Pearson frowned, but Monique could see the laughter dancing in his eyes.

"Aww, come on, babe. A little ding-a-ling swinging never hurt anybody."

"Oh I'll show you some ding-a-ling." Pearson pounced once again, and this time they made love until they exhausted themselves to sleep, then they woke up and started over again.

EPILOGUE

One year later...

"I can't believe this day has finally come. Girl, I think I'm more excited than you are." Venus was damn near jumping in her seat as she sipped her glass of champagne.

Monique laughed at her friend. "I think I've got you beat on the excitement. Now, last weekend was all you."

The weekend before, Venus had finally gotten her wish, she threw Monique the raunchiest bachelorette party in the history of bachelorette parties. They had everything from penis gag gifts to the infamous Mr. Hardcore. Venus was in hog heaven, and Monique hadn't laughed so hard in her entire life.

"Yes, I must thank your husband for letting Mr. Hardcore fulfill my fantasy all under the guise of having a party for you." Venus sighed her eyes glazing over. Monique could tell she had lost her friend to the memories of their wild night. Monique laughed and snapped her fingers in front of Venus' face to bring her back to the present.

"Alright, I think it's time I get into my gown. You ready?" Monique asked as she took a deep breath.

It was Valentine's Day, Monique and Pearson's wedding day.

Although they had been married well over a year, they'd decided to wait to have their wedding. Monique wanted to attend therapy for her family issues, and she wanted to make sure that she wasn't putting a strain on her relationship. Pearson agreed that therapy for her issues was good idea. They had even started going to a marriage counselor for extra support to make their relationship stronger.

Although Monique had put a lot of things behind her since she'd begun therapy, she still wasn't ready to have a relationship with her sister. Her forgiveness meter just wasn't high enough yet, so Ashley wasn't a part of her life at all. Monique still called her mother and talked to her once a week, but she no longer went to the disastrous dinners and she refused to give in to her mother's bullying ways.

Monique was in a much better place in her life, her career was amazing and after Pearson's glowing reviews, her clientele skyrocketed. Pearson's company was also doing fantastic. With Mark in prison and no longer able to sabotage Pearson's every move, the company was able to open their new division without any more delays. Keifer had even stepped up and taken the role of vice president.

After all of the things Mark had done had been revealed, Keifer wanted to make sure he was there for his friend. His past remarks against Pearson had come from Mark. Mark was trying to turn everyone in the company against Pearson, and if it weren't for Monique, it would've worked. Now, both of their companies were flourishing just like their love for one another.

Monique slid into her beautiful, off-white mermaid gown. The handmade crystal-embellished belt sparkled around her waist. The style complemented every dip and curve of Monique's physique. Her hair was pinned back into a sophisticated low chignon, and her matching veil was draped over her shoulders just right.

"You look gorgeous. Pearson is going to lose it," Venus said, wiping away tears.

"Don't start or I will have to redo my makeup, and ain't nobody got time for that."

The ladies laughed again.

"Alright, let's get this show on the road. Pearson is waiting, and I'm sure that fine ass Dom is out there somewhere. Hell, I'll even take surfer boy Keifer and turn him out."

Monique couldn't help the loud laughter that burst out of her. All tears were forgotten as she laughed with Venus. She was happy to be able to share such an important moment with her best friend.

PEARSON STOOD at the end of the short aisle in front of all of their friends and loved ones. The inside of the atrium garden was full of lush greenery even though it was mid-February. The aisle runner was white with pink and white candles lining the walkway. The pink and white pomanders were hanging from the backs of the chairs on the aisle, and the gazebo where Pearson stood was decorated with sheer white fabric and adorned with flowers and crystal hearts that sparkled under the candle light.

Dom stood beside Pearson in a sharp black suit that matched Pearson's. They adjusted their pink ties when the music started to play. Pearson took a deep breath and turned to watch his beautiful wife walk down the aisle toward him.

Monique was the epitome of exquisite as she floated toward him. Her off-white figure hugging dress made his breath catch. Her lovely heart-shaped face was covered by a lace veil, and he couldn't wait to lift it up, so that he could see her eyes.

Monique stopped in front of him, and the first thing he did was remove the veil.

"Pearson, you're supposed to wait." Monique giggled, but he could tell she didn't care.

"I've waited my entire life for you, I think that's long enough." Pearson winked, and Monique smiled widely. Before they knew it, the preacher was pronouncing them husband and wife... again. Pearson kissed Monique as if it were the only thing keeping him breathing.

"Wow!" Monique exclaimed once he pulled away from the kiss.

"Wow indeed Mrs. Grant." Pearson pecked her lips again before turning and jumping the broom. They walked down the aisle hand in hand to their happily ever after.

THE END

Want to be notified when the new, hot Urban Fiction and Interracial Romance books are released? Text the keyword "JWP" to 22828 to receive an email notifying you of new releases, giveaways, announcements, and more!

Made in the USA
Columbia, SC
13 February 2019